Catherine Winkworth

Lyra Germanica: Hymns for the Sundays

Chief Festivals of the Christian Year

Catherine Winkworth

Lyra Germanica: Hymns for the Sundays
Chief Festivals of the Christian Year

ISBN/EAN: 9783337076498

Printed in Europe, USA, Canada, Australia, Japan

Cover: Foto ©Andreas Hilbeck / pixelio.de

More available books at **www.hansebooks.com**

ANGELUS.

GERHARDT.

LUTHER.

Lyra Germanica

TERSTEEGEN.

SCHMOLCK.

HERMANN.

Lyra Germanica:

HYMNS FOR THE SUNDAYS
& CHIEF FESTIVALS
OF
THE CHRISTIAN YEAR.

TRANSLATED *from the* GERMAN *by* CATHERINE WINKWORTH.

With ILLUSTRATIONS *by and Engraved under the Superintendence of*
JOHN LEIGHTON, F.S.A.

LONDON:
LONGMAN, GREEN, LONGMAN, AND ROBERTS.
1861.

RICHARD CLAY
LONDON

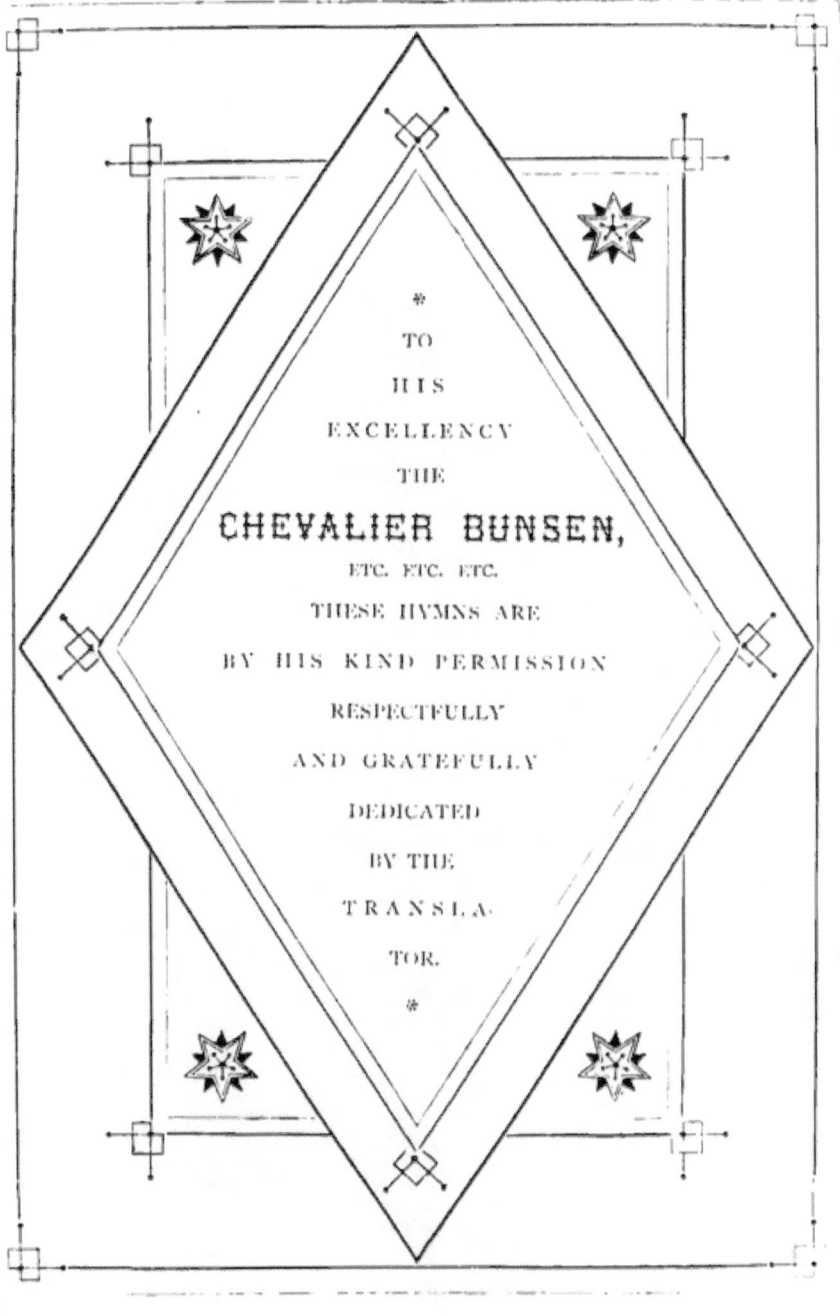

TO

HIS

EXCELLENCY

THE

CHEVALIER BUNSEN,

ETC. ETC. ETC.

THESE HYMNS ARE

BY HIS KIND PERMISSION

RESPECTFULLY

AND GRATEFULLY

DEDICATED

BY THE

TRANSLA-

TOR.

THE ENGRAVINGS

IN THIS VOLUME ARE EXECUTED BY

T. BOLTON, J. COOPER, G. & E. DALZIEL,

G. DE WILDE, W. GREEN, H. HARRAL, H. LEIGHTON,

W. MURDEN, G. PEARSON, and J. SWAIN,

FROM DESIGNS BY

E. ARMITAGE, pp. 29, 62, 111, 160, 167 ;

J. FLAXMAN, 114, 133 ; M. LAWLESS, 47, 90, 190 ;

C. KEENE, 182 ; S. MARKS, 1, 19, 57, 100 ;

and J. LEIGHTON.

PREFACE

The FOLLOWING HYMNS are selected from the Chevalier Bunsen's "Versuch eines allgemeinen Gesang und Gebetbuchs," published in 1833. From the large number there given, about nine hundred, little more than one hundred have been chosen. This selection contains many of those best known and loved in Germany; but in a work of this size it is impossible to include all that have become classical in that home of Christian poetry. In reading them it must be remembered that they are hymns, not sacred poems, though from their length and the intricacy of their metres, many of them may seem to English readers adapted rather to purposes of private than of public devotion. But the singing of hymns forms a much larger and more important part of public worship in the German Reformed Churches than in our own services. It is the mode by which the whole congregation is enabled to bear its part in the worship of God, answering in this respect to the chanting of our own Liturgy.

Ever since the Reformation, the German Church has been remarkable for the number and excellence of its hymns and hymn-tunes. Before that time it was not so. There was no place for congregational singing in public worship, and therefore the spiritual songs of the latter part of the middle ages assumed for the most part an artificial and unpopular form. Yet there were not wanting germs of a national Church poetry in the verses rather than hymns which were sung in German on pilgrimages and at some of the high festivals, many of which verses were again derived from more ancient Latin hymns. Several of Luther's hymns are amplifications of verses of this class, such as the Pentecostal hymn here given, " Come, Holy Spirit, God and Lord,"* which is founded on a German version of the " Veni Sancte Spiritus, Reple." By adopting these verses, and retaining their well-known melodies, Luther enabled his hymns to spread rapidly among the common people. He also composed metrical versions of several of the Psalms, the Te Deum, the Ten Commandments, the Lord's Prayer, the Nunc Dimittis, the Da nobis Pacem, &c., thus enriching the people, to whom he had already given the Holy Scriptures in their own language, with a treasure of that sacred poetry which is the precious inheritance of every Christian Church.

* Page 124.

PREFACE.

The hymn, "In the midst of life,"* is one of those founded on a more ancient hymn, the "Media in vita" of Notker, a learned Benedictine of St. Gall, who died in 912. He is said to have composed it while watching some workmen, who were building the bridge of Martinsbruck at the peril of their lives. It was soon set to music, and became universally known; indeed it was used as a battle song, until the custom was forbidden on account of its being supposed to exercise magical influences. In a German version it formed part of the service for the burial of the dead, as early as the thirteenth century, and is still preserved in an unmetrical form in the Burial Service of our own Church.

The carol, "From Heaven above to earth I come,"† is called by Luther himself, "A Christmas child's song concerning the child Jesus." He wrote it for his little boy Hans, when the latter was five years old, and it is still sung from the dome of the Kreuzkirche in Dresden before day-break on the morning of Christmas Day. It refers to the custom, then and long afterwards prevalent in Germany, of making at Christmas-time representations of the manger with the infant Jesus. But the most famous of his hymns is his noble version of the 46th Psalm, "A sure stronghold our God is He,"‡ which may be called the national hymn of his Protestant countrymen. Luther's hymns are wanting in harmony and correctness of metre to a degree which often makes them jarring to our modern ears, but they are always full of fire and strength, of clear Christian faith, and brave joyful trust in God.

* Page 245.   † Page 12.   ‡ Page 182.

From his time there has been a constant succession of hymn writers in the German Church. Paul Eber, an intimate friend of Melancthon, wrote for his children the hymn, "Lord Jesus Christ, true Man and God,"* which soon became a favourite hymn for the dying. Hugo Grotius asked that it might be repeated to him in his last moments, and expired ere its conclusion. Another hymn of the same class is, "Now hush your cries, and shed no tear,"† the "Jam mœsta quiesce querela" of Prudentius II. translated by Nicholas Hermann, the pious old precentor of Joachimsthal, a hymn long sung at every funeral.

The terrible times of the Thirty years' War were rich in sacred poetry. Rist, a clergyman in North Germany, who suffered much in his youth from mental conflicts, and in after years from plunder, pestilence, and all the horrors of war, used to say, "the dear cross hath pressed many songs out of me," and this seems to have been equally true of many of his contemporaries. It certainly was true of Johann Hermann, the author of some of the most touching hymns for Passion Week, who wrote his sweet songs under great physical sufferings from ill health, and amidst the perils of war, during which he more than once escaped murder as by a miracle. So too the hymns of Simon Dach,‡ professor of poetry in the University of Konigsberg, speak of the sufferings of the Christian, and his longing to escape from the strife of earth to the peace of heaven.

But the Christians of those days had often not only to suffer, but to fight for their faith, and in the hymns of

* Page 249.　　† Page 261.　　‡ Pages 136 and 265.

PREFACE.

Altenburgh and von Löwenstern we have two that may be called battle songs of the Church. The former published his hymn, "Fear not, O little flock, the foe,"* in 1631, with this title: "A heart-cheering song of comfort on the watch word of the Evangelical Army in the battle of Leipsic, September 7th, 1631, God with us." It was called Gustavus Adolphus' battle song, because the pious hero often sang it with his army; and he sang it for the last time immediately before the battle of Lützen. The latter, von Löwenstern, was the son of a saddler, but was ennobled by the Emperor, Ferdinand III. for his public services: he was at once a statesman, poet, and musician. His hymn, "Christ, Thou the champion of the band,"† was a favourite of Niebuhr.

Another favourite hymn of Niebuhr was the hymn to Eternity,‡ the greater part of which is of very ancient but uncertain date. It received its present form about the middle of the 17th century.

Many of the hymns of Paul Gerhardt belong to this period, though he lived until 1676, long after the conclusion of peace. He is without doubt the greatest of the German hymn writers, possessing loftier poetical genius, and a richer variety of thought and feeling than any other. His beautiful hymn, "Commit thou all thy ways," is already well known to us through Wesley's translation, and many others of his are not inferior to it. He was a zealous preacher for several years at the Nicolai-Kirch in Berlin; whence he retired because he had not sufficient freedom

* Page 18.   † Page 110.   ‡ Page 28.

in preaching the truth, and became Archdeacon of Lübben. With him culminated the elder school of German sacred poetry, a school distinguished by its depth and simplicity. Most of its hymns are either written for the high festivals and services of the Church, or are expressive of a simple Christian faith, ready to dare or suffer all things for God's sake. To this school we must refer, from their spirit, two hymns written a little later; the first is, "Jesus my Redeemer lives,"* one of the most favourite Easter hymns, written by the pious Electress of Brandenburgh, who founded the Orphan House at Oranienburg. The other, "Leave God to order all thy ways,"† was written by George Neumarck, Secretary to the Archives at Weimar. It spread rapidly among the common people, at first without the author's name. A baker's boy in New Brandenburgh used to sing it over his work, and soon the whole town and neighbourhood flocked to him to learn this beautiful new song.

In the latter half of the seventeenth century a new school was founded by Johann Franck, and Johann Scheffler, commonly called Angelus. The former was burgomaster of Guben in Lusatia; the latter physician to Ferdinand III.; but in 1663 he became a Roman Catholic, and afterwards a priest. The pervading idea of this school is the longing of the soul for that intimate union with the Redeemer of the world, which begins with the birth of Christ in the heart, and is perfected after death. This longing breathes through the hymns of Franck given in this collection; one of them, "Redeemer of the nations, come,"‡ is a translation of the "Veni, Redemptor gentium" of St. Ambrose.

* Page 97.   † Page 139.   ‡ Page 195.

Angelus dwells rather on the means of attaining this union by the sacrifice of the Self to God through the great High-priest of mankind, an idea expressed in his hymns with peculiar tenderness and sweetness. We find much of his spirit and sweetness lingering in modern times about the few hymns of the gifted Novalis.

The greatest poet of this school is however Gerhardt Tersteegen, who lived during the early part of the eighteenth century as a ribbon manufacturer at Mühlheim. His hymns have great beauty, and bespeak a tranquil and childlike soul filled and blessed with the contemplation of God. The well-known hymn of Wesley's, "Lo God is here! let us adore," belongs to him, and in its original shape is one of the most beautiful he ever wrote, but is frequently met with only in a disfigured and mutilated form. To this school belong a large number of the hymns in this collection, among which those of Deszler,* an excellent philologist of Nurem-burgh, and of Anton Ulrich,† the pious and learned Duke of Brunswick, are particularly good. Those of Schmolck, the pastor of Schweidnitz, who exercised great influence over the hymn-writing of his day, have more simplicity than most of the rest, but are characterized by a curious mixture of real poetry and deep feeling with occasional vulgarities of expression. The defects of this school, which showed themselves strongly in the course of the eighteenth century, were a tendency that the feeling should degenerate into sentimentality, and the devout dwelling of the heart on Christ's great sacrifice into compassion and gratitude for His physical sufferings,—defects which greatly disfigure many

* Pages 64 and 154.   † Pages 152, 167, and 229.

of the Moravian hymns. In some of the hymns here translated the expression "Christi Wundenhöhle" occurs, which
has been rendered by the blood or cross of Christ, as being
phrases at once more scriptural and more consonant to
our feelings. There were not wanting however, even at
this period, many hymns fit for good soldiers of Jesus Christ,
such as "Who seeks in weakness an excuse,"* and others
of the same kind.

Germany is rich in Morning and Evening Hymns, and
Hymns for the Dying, of which a few are given in these
translations. Among these is the morning hymn of Baron
von Canitz: I was not aware until after translating it that
it had been already published at the close of one volume
of Dr. Arnold's sermons.

The hymn "How blest to all Thy followers, Lord, the
road,"† was the favourite hymn of Schelling.

In translating these hymns the original form has been
retained, with the exception, that single rhymes are generally
substituted for the double rhymes which the structure of
the language renders so common in German poetry, but
which become cloying to an English ear when constantly
repeated ; and that English double common or short metre
is used instead of what may be called the German common
metre, the same that we call Gay's stanza, to which it approxi-
mates closely in the number of syllables, while its associations
in our minds are somewhat more solemn. In a few instances
slight alterations have been made in the metre, when, as is

* Page 156.   † Page 184.

the case with some excellent hymns in our own language,
it is hardly grave and dignified enough for the poetry.
These alterations are but slight, and seemed justifiable,
since these hymns have been translated, not so much as
specimens of German hymn-writing, as in the hope that
these utterances of Christian piety which have comforted
and strengthened the hearts of many true Christians in their
native country, may speak to the hearts of some among us,
to help and cheer those who must strive and suffer, and
to make us feel afresh what a deep and true Communion
of Saints exists among all the children of God in different
Churches and lands.

> Alderley Edge,
> July 16th,
> 1855.

In the second edition a few corrections have been made
and additional verses given in some of the hymns : a few
among them are however still given in an abbreviated
form, where the omitted verses appeared to be
decidely inferior in merit, or to contain no
new thought. I have also exchanged the
former version of " Ein feste Burg "
for one, as it seems to me, much
superior, which I owe to
the kindness of the
Rev. William
Gaskell.

Nov.
30,
1855.

CONTENTS.

CONTENTS.

CONTENTS.

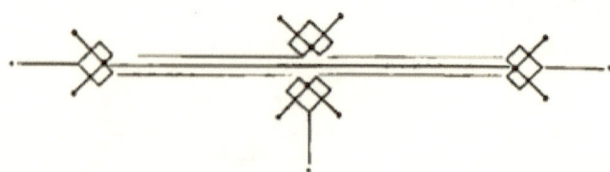

TRIANGLE — TRINITY.

Lyra Germanica

TIMBRIL — ETERNITY.

Except the LORD keep the City,
the Watchman waketh but in vain

LYRA GERMANICA

First Sunday in Advent.

The night is far spent, the day is at hand; let us therefore cast off the works of darkness, and let us put on the armour of light.   From the Epistle.

O WATCHMAN, will the night of sin
    Be never past?
O watchman, doth the tarrying day begin
To dawn upon thy straining sight at last?
    Will it dispel
Ere long the mists of sense wherein I dwell?

Now all the earth is bright and glad
    With the fresh morn;
But all my heart is cold and dark and sad;
Sun of the soul, let me behold Thy dawn!
    Come, Jesus, Lord!
Oh quickly come, according to Thy word!

Do we not live in those blest days
 So long foretold,
When Thou shouldst come to bring us light and
 grace ?
And yet I sit in darkness as of old,
 Pining to see
Thy glory ; but Thou still art far from me.

Long since Thou camest for the light
 Of all men here ;
And still in me is nought but blackest night.
Yet am I thine, Oh hasten to appear,
 Shine forth and bless
My soul with vision of Thy righteousness !

If thus in darkness ever left,
 Can I fulfil
The works of light, while yet of light bereft /
Or how discern in love and meekness still
 To follow Thee,
And all the sinful works of darkness flee ?

The light of reason cannot give
 Life to my soul ;
Jesus alone can make me truly live,
One glance of His can make my spirit whole.
 Arise, and shine,
O Jesus, on this longing heart of mine !

Single and clear, not weak or blind,
 The eye must be,

To which Thy glory shall an entrance find ;
For if Thy chosen ones would gaze on Thee,
    No earthly screen
Between their souls and Thee must intervene.

    Jesus, do Thou mine eyes unseal,
       And let them grow
    Quick to discern whate'er Thou dost reveal,
So shall I be deliver'd from that woe,
       Blindly to stray
Through hopeless night, while all around is day.

Second·Sunday·in·Advent

Behold the fig-tree and all the trees; when they now shoot forth, ye see and know of your own selves that summer is now nigh at hand. So likewise ye, when ye see these things come to pass, know ye that the kingdom of God is nigh at hand.

From the Gospel.

AWAKE, thou careless world, awake!
　　The final day shall surely come;
　What Heaven hath fix'd Time cannot
　　　　shake,
　It cannot sweep away thy doom.
Know, what the Lord Himself hath spoken
　　Shall come at last and not delay;
　　Though heaven and earth shall pass away,
　His steadfast word can ne'er be broken.

LYRA GERMANICA.

Awake ! He comes to judgment, wake !
  Sinners, behold His countenance
In beauty terrible, and quake
  Condemn'd beneath His piercing glance.
Lo ! He to whom all power is given,
  Who sits at God's right hand on high,
  In fire and thunder draweth nigh,
To judge all nations under Heaven.

Awake, thou careless world, awake !
  Who knows how soon our God shall please
That suddenly that day should break ?
  We fathom not such depths as these.
Oh guard thee well from lust and greed ;
  For as the bird is in the snare,
  Or ever of its foe aware,
So comes that day with silent speed.

The Lord in love delayeth long
  The final day, and grants us space
To turn away from sin and wrong,
  And mourning seek His help and grace.
He holdeth back that best of days,
  Until the righteous shall approve
  Their faith and hope, their constant love :
So gentle us-ward are His ways !

But ye, O faithful souls, shall see
  That morning rise in love and joy ;
Your Saviour comes to set you free,
  Your Judge shall all your bonds destroy :

He, the true Joshua, then shall bring
  His people with a mighty hand
  Into their promised father-land,
Where songs of victory they shall sing.

Rejoice ! the fig-tree shows her green,
  The springing year is in its prime,
The little flowers afresh are seen,
  We gather strength in this great time ;
The glorious summer draweth near,
  When all this body's earthly load,
  In light that morning sheds abroad,
Shall wax as sunshine pure and clear.

Arise, and let us day and night
  Pray in the Spirit ceaselessly,
That we may heed our Lord aright,
  And ever in His presence be ;
Arise, and let us haste to meet
  The Bridegroom standing at the door,
  That with the angels evermore
We too may worship at His feet.

Third Sunday in Advent

*And it shall be said in that day, Lo, this is our God;
we have waited for Him, and He will save us; this is
the Lord; we have waited for Him, we will be glad and
rejoice in His salvation.*   From the Lesson.

HOW shall I meet Thee? How my heart
   Receive her Lord aright?
Desire of all the earth Thou art!
   My hope, my sole delight!
Kindle the lamp, Thou Lord, alone,
  Half-dying in my breast,
And make thy gracious pleasure known
  How I may greet Thee best.

Her budding boughs and fairest palms
   Thy Zion strews around;
And songs of praise and sweetest psalms
   From my glad heart shall sound.
My desert soul breaks forth in flowers,
  Rejoicing in Thy fame:
And puts forth all her sleeping powers,
  To honour Jesus' name.

LYRA GERMANICA.

In heavy bonds I languish'd long,
  Thou com'st to set me free ;
The scorn of every mocking tongue—
  Thou com'st to honour me.
A heavenly crown wilt Thou bestow,
  And gifts of priceless worth,
That vanish not as here below
  The fading wealth of earth.

Nought, nought, dear Lord, had power to move
  Thee from Thy rightful place,
Save that most strange and blessed Love
  Wherewith Thou dost embrace
This weary world and all her woe,
  Her load of grief and ill
And sorrow, more than man can know ;—
  Thy love is deeper still.

Oh write this promise in your hearts,
  Ye sorrowful, on whom
Fall thickening cares, while joy departs
  And darker grows your gloom.
Despair not, for your help is near,
  He standeth at the door
Who best can comfort you and cheer,
  He comes, nor stayeth more.

Nor vex your souls with care, nor grieve
  And labour longer thus,
As though your arm could ought achieve,
  And bring Him down to us.

He comes, He comes with ready will,
  By pity moved alone,
To soothe our every grief and ill,
  For all to Him are known.

Nor ye, O sinners, shrink aside,
  Afraid to see His face,
Your darkest sins our Lord will hide
  Beneath His pitying grace.
He comes, He comes, to save from sin,
  And all its pangs assuage,
And for the sons of God to win
  Their proper heritage.

Why heed ye then the craft and noise,
  The fury of His foes?
Lo, in a breath the Lord destroys
  All who His rule oppose.
He comes, He comes, as King to reign!
  All earthly powers may band
Against Him, yet they strive in vain,
  His might may none withstand.

He comes to judge the earth, and ye
  Who mock'd Him, feel His wrath;
But they who loved and sought Him see
  His light o'er all their path.
O Sun of Righteousness! arise,
  And guide us on our way
To yon fair mansion in the skies
  Of joyous cloudless day.
                    PAUL GERHARDT. 1653.

Fourth Sunday in Advent

Rejoice in the Lord alway, and again I say, Rejoice.
The Lord is at hand.

From the Epistle.

LIFT up your heads, ye mighty gates,
Behold the King of glory waits,
The King of kings is drawing near,
The Saviour of the world is here ;
Life and salvation doth He bring,
Wherefore rejoice, and gladly sing
    Praise, O my God, to Thee !
    Creator, wise is Thy decree !

The Lord is just, a helper tried,
Mercy is ever at His side,
His kingly crown is holiness,
His sceptre, pity in distress,
The end of all our woe He brings ;
Wherefore the earth is glad and sings
    Praise, O my God, to Thee !
    O Saviour, great Thy deeds shall be !

Oh, blest the land, the city blest,
Where Christ the ruler is confest !
Oh, happy hearts and happy homes
To whom this King in triumph comes !
The cloudless Sun of joy He is,
Who bringeth pure delight and bliss ;
    Praise, O my God, to Thee !
    Comforter, for Thy comfort free !

Fling wide the portals of your heart,
Make it a temple set apart
From earthly use for Heaven's employ,
Adorn'd with prayer, and love, and joy;
So shall your Sovereign enter in,
And new and nobler life begin.
　　Praise, O my God, be Thine,
　　For word, and deed, and grace divine.

Redeemer, come! I open wide
My heart to Thee, here, Lord, abide!
Let me Thy inner presence feel,
Thy grace and love in me reveal,
Thy Holy Spirit guide us on
Until our glorious goal is won!
　　Eternal praise and fame,
　　Be offer'd, Saviour, to Thy Name!

WEISZEL.
1635.

LUTHER AND HIS LITTLE SON

𝕮𝖍𝖗𝖎𝖘𝖙𝖒𝖆𝖘 ✠ 𝕰𝖛𝖊

Behold, I bring you good tidings of great joy, which shall be to all people.
LUKE ii. 10.

ROM heaven above to earth I come
To bear good news to every home ;
Glad tidings ot great joy I bring,
Whereof I now will say and sing :

To you this night is born a child
Of Mary, chosen mother mild ;
This little child, of lowly birth,
Shall be the joy of all your earth.

'Tis Christ our God who far on high
Hath heard your sad and bitter cry :
Himself will your Salvation be,
Himself from sin will make you free.

He brings those blessings, long ago
Prepared by God for all below ;
Henceforth His kingdom open stands
To you, as to the angel bands.

These are the tokens ye shall mark,
The swaddling clothes and manger dark ;
There shall ye find the young child laid,
By whom the heavens and earth were made.

Now let us all with gladsome cheer
Follow the shepherds, and draw near
To see this wondrous gift of God
Who hath His only Son bestow'd.

Give heed, my heart, lift up thine eyes !
Who is it in yon manger lies ?
Who is this child so young and fair ?
The blessed Christ-child lieth there.

Welcome to earth, Thou noble guest,
Through whom e'en wicked men are blest !
Thou com'st to share our misery,
What can we render, Lord, to Thee !

Ah, Lord, who hast created all,
How hast Thou made Thee weak and small,
That Thou must choose Thy infant bed
Where ass and ox but lately fed !

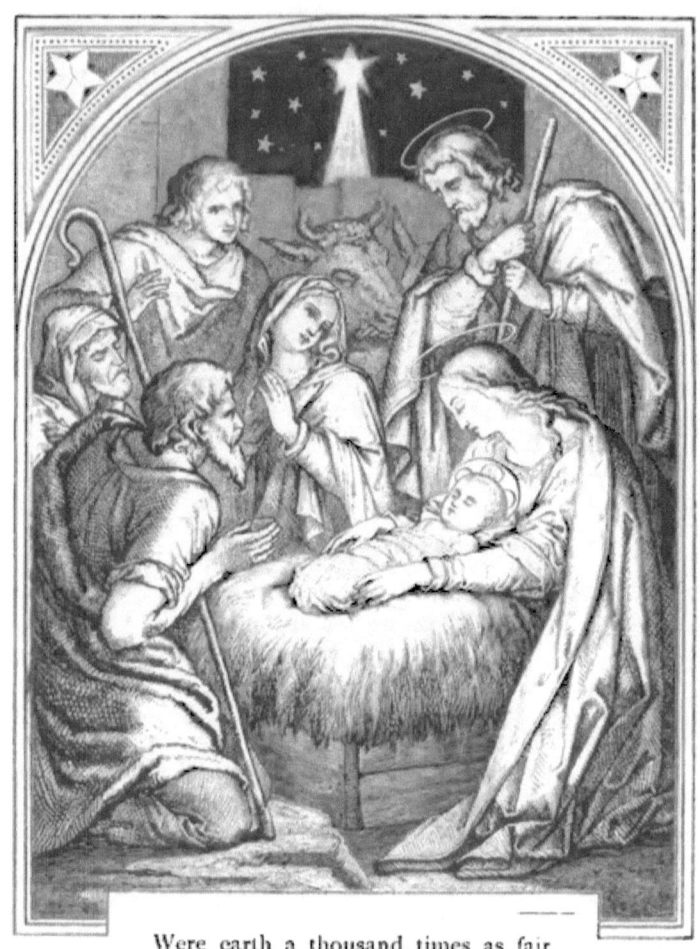

Were earth a thousand times as fair,
Beset with gold and jewels rare,
She yet were far too poor to be
A narrow cradle, Lord, for Thee.

For velvets soft and silken stuff
Thou hast but hay and straw so rough,
Whereon Thou King, so rich and great,
As 'twere Thy heaven, art throned in state.

Thus hath it pleas'd Thee to make plain
The truth to us poor fools and vain,
That this world's honour, wealth and might
Are nought and worthless in Thy sight.

Ah! dearest Jesus, Holy Child,
Make Thee a bed, soft, undefiled,
Within my heart, that it may be
A quiet chamber kept for Thee.

My heart for very joy doth leap,
My lips no more can silence keep ;
I too must sing with joyful tongue
That sweetest ancient cradle-song—

Glory to God in highest Heaven,
Who unto man His Son hath given !
While angels sing with pious mirth
A glad New Year to all the earth.

LUTHER.

Written for his little son Han

1540.

Xmas Day.

And the Word was made flesh, and dwelt among us.

From the Gospel.

O THOU essential Word,
　　Who from eternity
Didst dwell with God, for thou wast God,
　　Who art ordain'd to be
　　The Saviour of our race;
　　Welcome indeed Thou art,
Blessed Redeemer, Fount of Grace,
　　To this my longing heart !

Come, self-existent Word,
　　And speak within my heart,
That from the soul where Thou art heard
　　Thy peace may ne'er depart.
　　Thou Light that lightenest all.
　　Abide through faith in me,
And let me never from Thee fall,
　　And seek no guide but Thee.

Why didst Thou leave Thy throne.
　　O Jesus, what could bring
Thee to a world where e'en Thine own
　　Knew not their rightful King ?

Thy love beyond all thought
Stronger than Death or Hell,
And my deep woe, this wonder wrought,
That Thou on earth dost dwell.

Then help me, Lord, to give
My whole heart unto Thee,
That all my life while here I live
One song of praise may be.
Yes, Jesus, form anew
This stony heart of mine,
And let it e'en in death be true
To Thee, for ever Thine.

Let nought be left within
But cometh of Thy hand ;
Root quickly out the weeds of sin,
My cunning foe withstand.
From Thee comes nothing ill,
'Tis he doth sow the tares ;
Make plain my path before me still,
And save me from his snares.

Thou art the Life, O Lord !
Sole Light of Life Thou art !
Let not Thy glorious rays be pour'd
In vain on my dark heart.
Star of the East, arise !
Drive all my clouds away,
Guide me till earth's dim twilight dies
Into the perfect day !

LAURENTI. 1700.

St. Stephen's Day.

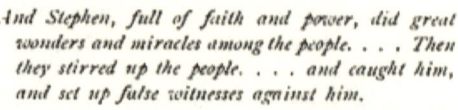

And Stephen, full of faith and power, did great
wonders and miracles among the people. . . . Then
they stirred up the people. . . . and caught him,
and set up false witnesses against him.

From the Lesson.

EAR not, O little flock, the foe
Who madly seeks your overthrow,
 Dread not his rage and power :
What though your courage sometimes faints,
His seeming triumph o'er God's saints
 Lasts but a little hour.

Be of good cheer ; your cause belongs
To Him who can avenge your wrongs,
 Leave it to Him our Lord.
Though hidden yet from all our eyes,
He sees the Gideon who shall rise
 To save us, and His word.

As true as God's own word is true,
Nor earth nor hell with all their crew
 Against us shall prevail.
A jest and by-word are they grown ;
God is with us, we are His own,
 Our victory cannot fail.

Amen, Lord Jesus, grant our prayer !
Great Captain, now Thine arm make bare ;
 Fight for us once again !

So shall Thy saints and martyrs raise
A mighty chorus to Thy praise,
   World without end. Amen.

ALTENBURG.

Gustavus Adolphus' Battle-song. 1631.

*If I will that ye tarry till
I come, what is that to
thee? Follow thou me.*
From the Gospel.

IF Thou, True Life, wilt in
  me live,
    Consume whate'er is not
      of Thee;
    One look of Thine more
      joy can give
  Than all the world can offer me.
O Jesus, be Thou mine for ever,
Nought from Thy love my heart
  can sever,
As Thou hast promised in Thy
  Word;
    Oh deep the joy whereof I
      drink,
    Whene'er my soul in Thee can
      sink,
And own her Bridegroom and her
  Lord!

O Heart, that glow'd with love and died,
  Kindle my soul with fire divine ;
Lord, in the heart Thou'st won, abide,
  And all in it that is not Thine
Oh let me conquer and destroy,
Strong in Thy love, Thou Fount of Joy,
Nay, be Thou conqueror, Lord, in me ;
  So shall I triumph o'er despair,
  O'er death itself Thy victory share,
Thus suffer, live, and die in Thee.

And let the fire within me move
  My heart to serve Thy members here :
Let me their need and trials prove,
  That I may know my love sincere
And like to Thine, Lord, pure and warm ;
For when my soul hath won that form
Is likest to Thy holy mind,
  Then I shall love both friends and foes,
  And learn to grieve o'er others' woes,
Like Thee, my Pattern, true and kind.

The light and strength of Faith, oh grant,
  That I may bring forth holy fruit,
A living branch, a blooming plant,
  Fast clinging to my vine—my root :

LYRA GERMANICA.

Thou art my Saviour, whom I trust,
My Rock,—I build not on the dust,—
The ground of faith, eternal, sure.
   When hours of doubt o'ercloud my mind,
   Thy ready help then let me find,
Thy strength my sickening spirit cure!

And grant that Hope may never fail,
   But anchor'd safely on Thy cross,
Through Thee who art mine All, prevail
   O'er every anguish, dread, and loss.
The world may build on what decays,
O Christ, my Sun of Hope, my gaze
Cares not o'er lesser lights to range;
   To Thee in love I ever cleave,
   For well I know Thou ne'er wilt leave
My soul,—Thy love can never change.

Wouldst Thou that I should tarry here,
   I live because Thou willest it;
Or Death should suddenly appear,
   I shall not fear him, Lord, one whit,
If but Thy life still in me live,
If but Thy death my strength shall give,
When earthly life draws near its end:
   To Thee I give away my will,
   In life and death remembering still
Thou wilt my good, O truest Friend.

SINOLD.

1712.

INNOCENTS · DAY ·

Except ye be converted, and become as little children, ye shall not enter into the kingdom of Heaven.

Matt. xviii. 3.

DEAR Soul, couldst thou become a child
While yet on earth, meek, undefiled,
Then God Himself were ever near,
And Paradise around thee here.

A child cares nought for gold or treasure,
Nor fame nor glory yield him pleasure;
In perfect trust, he asketh not
If rich or poor shall be his lot.

Little he recks of dignity,
Nor prince nor monarch feareth he;
Strange that a child so weak and small
Is oft the boldest of us all!

He hath not skill to utter lies,
His very soul is in his eyes;
Single his aim in all, and true,
And apt to praise what others do.

No questions dark his spirit vex,
No faithless doubts his soul perplex,
Simply from day to day he lives,
Content with what the present gives.

Scarce can he stand alone, far less
Would roam abroad in loneliness;
Fast clinging to his mother still,
She bears and leads him at her will.

He will not stay to pause and choose,
His father's guidance e'er refuse,
Thinks not of danger, fears no harm,
Wrapt in obedience' holy calm.

For strange concerns he careth nought;
What others do, although were wrought
Before his eyes the worst offence,
Stains not his tranquil innocence.

His dearest work, his best delight,
Is, lying in his mother's sight,
To gaze for ever on her face,
And nestle in her fond embrace.

O childhood's innocence! the voice
Of thy deep wisdom is my choice!
Who hath thy lore is truly wise,
And precious in our Father's eyes.

Spirit of childhood! loved of God,
By Jesu's Spirit now bestow'd;
How often have I long'd for thee;
O Jesus, form Thyself in me!

And help me to become a child
While yet on earth, meek, undefiled,
That I may find God always near,
And Paradise around me here.

GERHARDT TERSTEEGEN.

1731.

SUNDAY AFTER CHRISTMAS-DAY.

*Behold, a Virgin shall be with child, and shall
bring forth a Son, and they shall call his
name Emmanuel, which being interpreted
is, God with us.*

From the Gospel.

HEE, O Immanuel, we praise,
The Prince of Life, and Fount of Grace,
The Morning Star, the Heavenly Flower,
The Virgin's Son, the Lord of Power.

With all Thy saints, Thee, Lord, we sing,
Praise, honour, thanks to Thee we bring,
That Thou, O long-expected guest,
Hast come at last to make us blest!

Since first the world began to be,
How many a heart hath long'd for Thee;
Long years our fathers hoped of old
Their eyes might yet Thy Light behold:

The prophets cried; "Ah, would He came
To break the fetters of our shame;
That help from Zion came to men,
Israel were glad, and prosper'd then!"

LYRA GERMANICA.

Now art Thou here; we know Thee now,
In lowly manger liest Thou;
A child, yet makest all things great,
Poor, yet is earth Thy robe of state.

From Thee alone all gladness flows,
Who yet shalt bear such bitter woes;
Earth's light and comfort Thou shalt be,
Yet none shall watch to comfort Thee.

All heavens are Thine, yet Thou dost come
To sojourn in a stranger's home;
Thou hangest on Thy mother's breast
Who art the joy of spirits blest.

Now fearless I can look on Thee,
From sin and grief Thou sett'st me free:
Thou bearest wrath, Thou conquerest Death,
Fear turns to joy Thy glance beneath.

Thou art my Head, my Lord Divine,
I am Thy member, wholly Thine,
And in Thy Spirit's strength would still
Serve Thee according to Thy will.

Thus will I sing Thy praises here
With joyful spirit year by year;
And they shall sound before Thy throne,
Where time nor number more are known.

PAUL GERHARDT. 1650.

The Circumcision of Christ.

HYMN FOR NEW YEAR'S DAY.

So teach us to number our days, that we may apply our hearts unto wisdom.   Psalm xc. 12.

ETERNITY!
    How long art thou, Eternity!
And yet to thee Time hastes away,
Like as the warhorse to the fray,
Or swift as couriers homeward go,
Or ship to port, or shaft from bow.
Ponder, O Man, Eternity!

Eternity! Eternity!
How long art thou, Eternity!
For even as on a perfect sphere
End nor beginning can appear,
Even so, Eternity, in thee
Entrance nor exit can there be.
Ponder, O Man, Eternity!

Eternity! Eternity!
How long art thou, Eternity!
A circle infinite art thou,
Thy centre an Eternal Now,
Never, we name thy outer bound,
For never end therein is found.
Ponder, O Man, Eternity!

Eternity! Eternity!
How long art thou, Eternity!
A little bird with fretting beak
Might wear to nought the loftiest peak.

Though but each thousand years it came,
Yet thou wert then, as now, the same.
Ponder, O Man, Eternity!

LYRA GERMANICA.

Eternity! Eternity!
How long art thou, Eternity!
As long as God is God, so long
Endure the pains of sin and wrong,
So long the joys of heaven remain;
Oh lasting joy, Oh lasting pain!
Ponder, O Man, Eternity!

Eternity! Eternity!
How long art thou, Eternity!
O Man, full oft thy thoughts should dwell
Upon the pains of sin and hell,
And on the glories of the pure,
That both beyond all time endure.
Ponder, O Man, Eternity!

Eternity! Eternity!
How long art thou, Eternity!
How terrible art thou in woe,
How fair where joys for ever glow!
God's goodness sheddeth gladness here,
His justice there wakes bitter fear.
Ponder, O Man, Eternity!

Eternity! Eternity!
How long art thou, Eternity!
They who lived poor and naked rest
With God, for ever rich and blest,
And love and praise the Highest Good,
In perfect bliss and gladsome mood.
Ponder, O Man, Eternity!

Eternity ! Eternity !
How long art thou, Eternity !
A moment lasts all joy below,
Whereby man sinks to endless woe,
A moment lasts all earthly pain,
Whereby an endless joy we gain.
Ponder, O Man, Eternity !

Eternity ! Eternity !
How long art thou, Eternity !
Who ponders oft on thee, is wise,
All fleshly lusts will he despise,
The world finds place with him no more ;
The love of vain delights is o'er.
Ponder, O Man, Eternity !

Eternity ! Eternity !
How long art thou, Eternity !
Who marks thee well would say to God,
Here judge, burn, smite me with Thy rod,
Here let me all Thy justice bear,
When time of grace is past, then spare !
Ponder, O Man, Eternity !

Eternity ! Eternity !
How long art thou, Eternity !
Lo, I, Eternity, warn thee,
O Man, that oft thou think on me,
The sinner's punishment and pain,
To them who love their God, rich gain !
Ponder, O Man, Eternity !

WÜLFFER.   1648.

THE ADORATION OF THE MAGI

EPIPHANY.

Arise, shine, for thy light is come, and the glory of the Lord is risen upon thee!

From the Lesson.

ALL ye Gentile lands awake!
    Thou, O Salem, rise and shine!
See the day spring o'er you break,
Heralding a morn divine,
Telling, God hath call'd to mind
Those who long in darkness pined.

Lo! the shadows flee away,
    For our Light is come at length,
Brighter than all earthly day,
    Source of being, life, and strength!
Whoso on this Light would gaze
Must forsake all evil ways.

Ah how blindly did we stray
  Ere shone forth this glorious Sun,
Seeking each his separate way,
  Leaving Heaven, unsought, unwon ;
All our looks were earthward bent,
All our strength on earth was spent.

Earthly were our thoughts and low,
  In the toils of Folly caught,
Toss'd of Satan to and fro,
  Counting goodness all for nought ;
By the world and flesh deceived,
Heaven's true joys we disbelieved.

Then were hidden from our eyes
  All the law and grace of God ;
Rich and poor, the fools and wise,
  Wanting light to find the road
Leading to the heavenly life,
Wander'd lost in care and strife.

But the glory of the Lord
  Hath arisen on us to-day,
We have seen the light outpour'd
  That must surely drive away
All things that to night belong,
All the sad earth's woe and wrong.

Thy arising, Lord, shall fill
  All my thoughts in sorrow's hour;
Thy arising, Lord, shall still
  All my dread of Death's dark power:
Through my smiles and through my tears
Still Thy light, O Lord, appears.

Let me, Lord, in peace depart
  From this evil world to Thee;
Where Thyself sole Brightness art,
  Thou hast kept a place for me:
In the shining city there
Crowns of light Thy saints shall wear.

R I   S T

1655

First Sunday after Epiphany

I beseech you therefore, brethren, by the mercies of God, that ye present your bodies a living sacrifice, holy, acceptable unto God, which is your reasonable service. From the Epistle.

GREAT High-priest, who deign'dst to be
  Once the sacrifice for me,
Take this living heart of mine,
Lay it on Thy holy shrine.

LOVE I know accepteth nought,
  Save what Thou, O Love, hast wrought :
Offer Thou my sacrifice,
Else to God it cannot rise.

SLAY in me the wayward will,
  Earthly sense and passion kill,
Tear self-love from out my heart,
Though it cost me bitter smart.

KINDLE, Mighty Love, the pyre,
  Quick consume me in Thy fire,
Fain were I of self bereft,
Nought but Thee within me left.

SO MAY God, the Righteous, brook
  On my sacrifice to look ;
In whose sight no gift has worth
Save a Christ-like life on earth.

ANGELUS.
1647.

35

Second Sunday after Epiphany.

LIFT up your eyes unto the heavens, and look upon the earth beneath; for the heavens shall vanish away like smoke, and the earth shall wax old like a garment, and the people that dwell therein shall die in like manner; but my salvation shall be for ever, and my righteousness shall not be abolished.

From the Lesson.

GOD liveth ever!
Wherefore, Soul, despair thou never!
Our God is good, in every place
His love is known, His help is found,
His mighty arm, and tender grace
  Bring good from ills that hem us round;
  Easier than we think can He
  Turn to joy our agony;
  Soul, remember 'mid thy pains,
  God o'er all for ever reigns.

God liveth ever!
Wherefore, Soul, despair thou never!
Say, shall He slumber, shall He sleep,
Who gave the eye its power to see?
Shall He not hear His children weep
  Who made the ear so wondrously?
  God is God; He sees and hears
  All their troubles, all their tears.
  Soul, forget not 'mid thy pains,
  God o'er all for ever reigns.

36

God liveth ever!
Wherefore, Soul, despair thou never!
He who can earth and heaven control,
  Who spreads the clouds o'er sea and land,
Whose presence fills the mighty Whole,
  In each true heart is close at hand;
    Love Him, He will surely send
    Help and joy that never end.
    Soul, remember in thy pains,
    God o'er all for ever reigns.

God liveth ever!
Wherefore, Soul, despair thou never!
Scarce canst thou bear thy cross? Then fly
  To Him where only rest is sweet;
Thy God is great, His mercy nigh,
  His strength upholds the tottering feet:
    Trust Him, for His grace is sure,
    Ever doth His truth endure;
    Soul, forget not in thy pains,
    God o'er all for ever reigns.

God liveth ever!
Wherefore, Soul, despair thou never!
When sins and follies long forgot
  Upon thy tortured conscience prey,
Oh come to God, and fear Him not,
  His love shall sweep them all away;
    Pains of hell at look of His,
    Change to calm content and bliss.
    Soul, remember in thy pains,
    God o'er all for ever reigns.

God liveth ever!
Wherefore, Soul, despair thou never!
Those whom the thoughtless world forsakes,
Who stand bewilder'd with their woe,
God gently to His bosom takes,
And bids them all His fulness know;
In thy sorrows' swelling flood
Own His hand who seeks thy good.
Soul, forget not in thy pains,
God o'er all for ever reigns.

God liveth ever!
Wherefore, Soul, despair thou never!
Let earth and heaven outworn with age,
Sink to the chaos whence they came;
Let angry foes against us rage,
Let hell shoot forth his fiercest flame;
Fear not Death, nor Satan's thrusts,
God defends who in Him trusts;
Soul, remember in thy pains,
God o'er all for ever reigns.

God liveth ever!
Wherefore, Soul, despair thou never!
What though thou tread with bleeding feet
A thorny path of grief and gloom,
Thy God will choose the way most meet
To lead thee heavenwards, lead thee home.
For this life's long night of sadness
He will give thee peace and gladness:
Soul, remember in thy pains,
God o'er all for ever reigns.

ZIHN. 1682.

Third Sunday After Epiphany

For as the rain cometh down, and the snow from heaven; and returneth
not thither, but watereth the earth, and maketh it bring forth and bud,
that it may give seed to the sower, and bread to the eater; so
shall my word be that goeth forth out of my mouth; it shall
not return unto me void, but it shall accomplish that which
I please, and it shall prosper in the thing whereto I sent it.

From the Lesson.

THY Word, O Lord, like gentle dews,
　　Falls soft on hearts that pine;
Lord, to Thy garden ne'er refuse
　　This heavenly balm of Thine.
　　　　Water'd from Thee
　　　　Let every tree
Bud forth and blossom to Thy praise,
And bear much fruit in after days.

Thy word is like a flaming sword,
　　A wedge that cleaveth stone;
Keen as a fire so burns Thy Word,
　　And pierceth flesh and bone.

Oh send it forth
O'er all the earth,
To shatter all the might of sin,
The darken'd heart to cleanse and win.

Thy Word a wondrous guiding star,
On pilgrim hearts doth rise,
Leads to their Lord who dwell afar,
And makes the simple wise.
Let not its light
E'er sink in night,
But still in every spirit shine,
That none may miss Thy light divine.

ANON.

Fourth Sunday After Epiphany

And He saith unto them, Why are ye fearful, O ye
of little faith? Then He arose and rebuked the winds
and the sea, and there was a great calm.

From the Gospel.

MY GOD, lo, here before Thy face
    I cast me in the dust;
Where is the hope of happier days,
    Where is my wonted trust?
Where are the sunny hours I had
    Ere of Thy light bereft?
Vanish'd is all that made me glad,
    My pain alone is left.

I shrink with fear and sore alarm
    When threatening ills I see.
As though in time of need Thine arm
    No more could shelter me:

As though Thou couldst not see the grief
   That makes my courage quail,
As though Thou wouldst not send relief,
   When human helpers fail.

Cannot Thy might avert e'en now
   What seems my certain doom,
And still with light and succour bow
   To him who weeps in gloom?
Art Thou not evermore the same?
   And hast not Thou revealed
That Thou wilt be our strength, Thy Name
   Our tower of hope, our shield?

O Father, compass me about
   With love, for I am weak;
Forgive, forgive my sinful doubt,
   Thy pitying glance I seek;
For torn and anguish'd is my heart,
   Thou seest it, my God,
Oh soothe my conscience' bitter smart,
   Lift off my sorrows' load.

I know that I am in Thy hands,
   Whose thoughts are peace toward me,
That ever sure Thy counsel stands,—
   Could I but build on Thee!
I know that Thou wilt give me all
   That Thou hast promised, Lord;
Here will I cling, nor yield, nor fall,
   I live but by Thy Word.

Though mountains crumble into dust,
   Thy covenant standeth fast ;
Who follows Thee in pious trust
   Shall reach the goal at last.
Though strange and winding seem the way
   While yet on earth I dwell,
In heaven my heart shall gladly say,
   Thou, God, dost all things well !

Take courage then, my soul, nor steep
   Thy days and nights in tears,
Thou soon shalt cease to mourn and weep,
   Though dark are now thy fears.
He comes, He comes, the Strong to save,
   He comes nor tarries more,
His light is breaking o'er the wave,
   The clouds and storms are o'er !

Fifth Sunday
after Epiphany.

*Oh that Thou wouldest rend the heavens, that Thou wouldest
come down, that the mountains might flow down at Thy
presence . . . To make Thy name known to Thine adver-
saries, that the nations may tremble at Thy
presence.*

From the Lesson.

AWAKE Thou Spirit, who of old
    Didst fire the watchmen of
        the Church's youth,
Who faced the foe, unshrinking, bold,
Who witness'd day and night the eternal
        truth,
Whose voices through the world are ringing
        still,
And bringing hosts to know and do Thy
        will !

Oh that Thy fire were kindled soon,
That swift from land to land its flame might
        leap !
Lord, give us but this priceless boon
Of faithful servants, fit for Thee to reap
The harvest of the soul ; look down and view
How great the harvest, yet the labourers
        few.

Lord, let our earnest prayer be heard,
The prayer Thy Son Himself hath bid us pray ;
For, lo ! Thy children's hearts are stirr'd

In every land in this our darkening day,
To cry for help with fervent soul to Thee ;
Oh hear us, Lord, and speak, Thus let it be !

Oh haste to help ere we are lost !
Send forth evangelists, in spirit strong,
Arm'd with Thy Word, a dauntless host,
Bold to attack the rule of ancient wrong,
And let them all the earth for Thee reclaim,
To be Thy kingdom, and to know Thy name.

Would there were help within our walls !
Oh let Thy promised Spirit come again,
Before whom every barrier falls,
And ere the night once more shine forth as then !
Oh rend the heavens and make Thy presence felt,
The chains that bind us at Thy touch would melt !

And let Thy Word have speedy course,
Through every land the truth be glorified,
Till all the heathen know its force,
And gather to Thy churches far and wide ;
And waken Israel from her sleep, O Lord !
Thus bless and spread the conquests of Thy Word !

The Church's desert paths restore,
That stumbling blocks which long in them have lain.
May hinder now Thy Word no more ;
Destroy false doctrine, root out notions vain,
Set free from hirelings, let the Church and school
Bloom as a garden 'neath Thy prospering rule !

BOGATZKY. 1727.

Sixth Sunday after Epiphany.

EVERY man that hath this hope in him
purifieth himself even as He is pure.

From the Epistle.

PURE Essence! Spotless Fount of Light,
　　That fadeth never into dark!
O Thou, whose eyes more clear and bright
　　Than noonday sun are quick to mark
Our sins; lo, bare before Thy face
　　Lies all the desert of my heart,
　　My once fair soul in every part
Now stain'd with evil foul and base.

Since but the pure in heart are blest
　　With promised vision of their God,
Sore fear and anguish fill my breast,
　　Rememb'ring all the ways I trod;
Mourning I see my lost estate,
　　And yet in faith I dare to cry,
　　Oh let my evil nature die,
Another heart in me create!

Enough, Lord, that my foe too well
　　Hath lured me once away from Thee;
Henceforth I know his craft how fell,
　　And all his deep-laid snares I flee.
Lord, through the Spirit whom Thy Son
　　Hath bidden us in prayer to ask,
　　Arm us with might that every task,
Whate'er we do, in Thee be done.

46

Unworthy am I of Thy grace,
  So deep are my transgressions, Lord,
And yet once more I seek Thy face;
  My God, have mercy, nor reward
My sins and follies, dark and vain;
  Reject, reject me not in wrath,
  But let Thy sunshine now beam forth,
And quicken me with hope again.

The Holy Spirit Thou hast given,
 The wondrous pledge of love divine,
Who fills our hearts with joys of heaven,
 And bids us earthly joys resign ;
Oh let His seal be on my heart,
 Oh take Him nevermore away,
 Until this fleshly house decay,
And Thou shalt bid me hence depart.

But ah ! my coward spirit droops,
 Sick with the fear that enters in
Whene'er a soul to bondage stoops,
 And wears the shameful yoke of sin ;
Oh quicken with the strength that flows
 From out the Eternal Fount of Life,
 My soul half-fainting in the strife,
And make an end of all my woes.

I cling unto Thy grace alone,
 Thy steadfast oath my only rest ;
To Thee, Heart-searcher, all is known
 That lieth hidden in my breast ;
Thy joy, O Spirit, on me pour,
 Thy fervent will my sloth inspire,
 So shall I have my heart's desire,
And serve and praise Thee evermore.

FREYLINGHAUSEN.

1713.

Septuagesima Sunday.

I therefore so run, not as uncertainly; so fight I, not as one that beateth the air.

From the Epistle.

STRIVE when thou art call'd of God,
　When He draws thee by his grace,
Strive to cast away the load
　That would clog thee in the race!

Fight, though it may cost thy life;
　Storm the kingdom, but prevail;
Let not Satan's fiercest strife
　Make thee, warrior, faint or quail.

Wrestle, till through every vein
　Love and strength are glowing warm,
Love that can the world disdain,
　Half-love will not bide the storm.

Wrestle with strong prayers and cries,
　Think no time too much to spend,
Though the night be pass'd in sighs,
　Though all day thy voice ascend.

Hast thou won the pearl of price,
    Think not thou hast reach'd the goal,
Conquer'd every sin and vice
    That had power to harm thy soul.

Gaze with mingled joy and fear
    On the refuge thou hast found ;
Know, while yet we linger here
    Perils ever hem us round.

Art thou faithful ? then oppose
    Sin and wrong with all thy might ;
Care not how the tempest blows,
    Only care to win the fight.

Art thou faithful ? Wake and watch,
    Love with all thy heart Christ's ways,
Seek not transient ease to snatch,
    Look not for reward or praise.

Art thou faithful ? Stand apart
    From all worldly hope and pleasure,
Yonder fix thy hopes and heart,
    On the heaven where lies our treasure.

Soldiers of the Cross, be strong,
    Watch and war 'mid fear and pain,
Daily conquering woe and wrong,
    Till our King o'er earth shall reign !

WINKLER.   1703.

Septuagesima Sunday.

Let them praise the name of the Lord: for His name alone is excellent: His glory is above the earth and heaven.

NOTHING fair on earth I see
But I straightway think on Thee;
Thou art fairest in mine eyes,
Source in whom all beauty lies!

When the golden sun forth goes,
And the east before him glows,
Quickly turns this heart of mine
To Thy heavenly form divine.

On Thy light I think at morn,
With the earliest break of dawn;
Ah, what glories lie in Thee,
Light of all Eternity!

When I watch the moon arise
'Mid Heaven's thousand golden eyes.
Then I think, more glorious far
Is the Maker of yon star.

Or I cry in spring's sweet hours,
When the fields are gay with flowers,
As their varied hues I see,
What must their Creator be !

When along the brook I wander,
Or beside the fountain ponder,
Straight my thoughts take wing and
    mount
Up to Thee, the purest Fount.

Sweetly sings the nightingale,
Sweet the flute's soft plaintive tale,
Sweeter than their richest tone,
Is the name of Mary's Son.

Sweetly all the air is stirr'd
When the Echo's call is heard ;
But no sounds my heart rejoice
Like to my Beloved's voice.

Come then, fairest Lord, appear,
Come, let me behold Thee here,
I would see Thee face to face,
On Thy proper light would gaze.

Take away these veils that blind,
Jesus, all my soul and mind ;
Henceforth ever let my heart
See Thee truly as Thou art !

                ANGELUS. 1657.

Quinquagesima Sunday.

*And now abideth faith, hope, charity, these three;
but the greatest of these is charity.*

From the Epistle.

MANY a gift did Christ impart,
  Noblest of them all is Love;
  Love, a balm within the heart
That can all its pains remove;
  Love, a star most bright and pure;
  Love, a gem of priceless worth,
  Richer than man knows on earth;
Love, like beauty, strong to lure;
  Love, like joy, makes man her thrall.
  Strong to please and conquer all.

Love can give us all things; here
  Use and beauty cannot sever;
Love can raise us to that sphere
  Whence the soul tends heavenwards ever;
Though one speak with angel tongues
  Bravest words of strength and fire,
  If no love his heart inspire,
They are but as fleeting songs;
  All his eloquence shall pass,
  As the noise of sounding brass.

Science with her keen-eyed glance,
　All the wisdom of the world,
Mysteries that the soul entrance,
　Faith that mighty hills had hurl'd
From their ancient seats;—all this,
　Wherein man takes most his pride,
　Valueless is cast aside,
If the spirit there we miss,
　That can work from love alone,
　Not from pride in what is known.

Though I lavish'd all I have
　On the poor in charity;
Though I shrank not from the grave,
　Or unmoved the stake could see;
Though my body here were given
　To the all-consuming flame;
　If my mind were still the same,
Meeter were I not for heaven,
　Till by Love my works were crown'd,
　Till in Love my strength were found.

Faith must conquer, Hope must bloom,
　As our onward path we wend,
Else we came not through the gloom,
　But with earth they also end :
Thou, O Love, doth stretch afar
　Through the wide eternity,
　And the soul array'd in Thee
Shines for ever as a star.
　Faith and Hope must pass away,
　Thou, O Love, endurest aye.

Come, thou Spirit of pure Love,
  Who dost forth from God proceed,
Never from my heart remove,
  Let me all Thy impulse heed;
All that seeks self-profit first,
  Rather than another's good,
  Whether foe or link'd in blood,
Let me hold such thought accurst;
  And my heart henceforward be
  Ruled, inspired, O Love, by thee!

               ERNST LANGE. 1711.

QUINQUAGESIMA SUNDAY.

And Jesus said unto him, Receive thy sight; thy faith hath saved thee.
And immediately he received his sight, and followed him, glorifying God.
From the Gospel.

MY Saviour, what Thou didst of old,
  When thou wast dwelling here,
Thou doest yet for them, who bold
  In faith to Thee draw near.
As thou hadst pity on the blind,
  According to Thy Word,
Thou sufferedst me Thy grace to find,
  Thy Light hast on me pour'd.

Mourning I sat beside the way,
  In sightless gloom apart,
And sadness heavy on me lay,
  And longing gnaw'd my heart :
I heard the music of the psalms
  Thy people sang to Thee,
I felt the waving of their palms,
  And yet I could not see.

My pain grew more than I could bear,
  Too keen my grief became,
Then I took heart in my despair
  To call upon Thy name ;
"O Son of David, save and heal,
  As Thou so oft hast done !
O dearest Jesus, let me feel
  My load of darkness gone."

And ever weeping as I spoke
   With bitter prayers and sighs,
My stony heart grew soft and broke.
   More earnest yet my cries.

LYRA GERMANICA.

A sudden answer still'd my fear,
    For it was said to me,
"O poor blind man, be of good cheer,
    Rejoice, He calleth thee."

I felt, Lord, that Thou stoodest still,
    Groping Thy feet I sought,
From off me fell my old self-will,
    A change came o'er my thought.
Thou saidst, "What is it thou wouldst have?"
    "Lord, that I might have sight ;
To see Thy countenance I crave :"
    "So be it, have thou Light."

And words of Thine can never fail,
    My fears are past and o'er ;
My soul is glad with light, the veil
    Is on my heart no more.
Thou blessest me, and forth I fare
    Free from my old disgrace,
And follow on with joy where'er
    Thy footsteps, Lord, I trace.

DE LA MOTHE FOQUÉ.

ASH WEDNESDAY.

*Gather the people . . and let the priests, the
ministers of the Lord, weep between the porch
and the altar, and let them say, Spare Thy
people, O Lord.*

From the Passage for the Epistle.

NOT in anger smite us, Lord,
Spare Thy people, spare !
If Thou mete us due reward
We must all despair.
Let the flood
Of Jesus' blood
Quench the flaming of Thy wrath,
That our sin enkindled hath.

Father ! Thou hast patience long
With the sick and weak ;
Heal us, make us brave and strong,
Words of comfort speak.
Touch my soul,
And make me whole
With Thy healing precious balm ;
Ward off all would bring me harm.

Weary am I, Lord, and worn
With my ceaseless pain ;
Sad the heart that night and morn
Sighs for help in vain.

Wilt Thou yet
My soul forget,
Waiting anxiously for Thee
In the cave of misery?

Hence, ye foes! God hears my prayer
From His holy place;
Once again with hope I dare
Come before His face.
Satan flee,
Hell touch not me;
God hath given me power o'er all,
Who once mock'd and sought my fall.

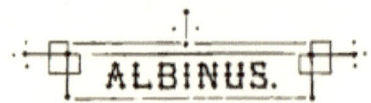

ALBINUS.

1652.

First Sunday in Lent.

Then was Jesus led up of the Spirit into the wilderness to be tempted of the devil. And he fasted forty days and forty nights.

From the Gospel.

AM I a stranger here, on earth alone,
When shall my weary days be past and gone?
When shall I find some respite, some relief
From this unsleeping pain, this haunting grief?

The joyful sun another morning brings,
I only wake to feel care's piercing stings;
The soft moon comes with silent night and sleep,
And bringeth nought to me but time to weep.

My heart and conscience sorely wounded lie,
Struck by the arrows of Thy wrath, Most High!
From morn till eventide where'er I flee,
I find no hiding-place, great God, from Thee!

O Lord, be not so strict to mark my crimes!
Great God, dost thou remember yet those times
Of foolish thoughtlessness, when blind and young
My heart to vain delights of earth still clung!

Wilt Thou then alway bear my sins in mind?
What offering, what atonement can I find!
Nought have I of mine own but sin and wrong.
But love and mercy, Lord, to Thee belong!

Oh therefore leave me not the wretched prey
Of those who seek to take my life away!
Yet though with streaming eyes to Thee I cry,
No answering voice comes from Thy throne on high.

Vain are my tears and prayers, vain all my woe,
While Thou dost fight against me as a foe;
The zeal of Thy just anger and Thy might
Have plunged my soul in blackest depths of night.

I sit alone; with tears I bathe my cheeks,
With bitter sighs and groans my spirit seeks
For Him, who veils behind the clouds His face,
And hears not, as of old in happier days.

Oh that I had a dove's swift wings! I'd fly
Away to some far mountain lone and high,—
Yet could I not escape His mighty hand
Before whom all things bare and open stand.

Nay, rather let me suffer all His will,
Though His fierce anger beat upon me still,
A willing heart and patient mind, O God!
I bring to Thy severe but righteous rod.

Much have I sinn'd, I perish utterly
If my misdeeds be all avenged of Thee;
Yet, Lord of Hosts, doth not thy Word proclaim,
The Merciful is Thy most glorious name!

RAISNER. 1678.

SECOND SUNDAY IN LENT.

And the disciples said, Send her away, for she crieth after us; . . .
But He said, Great is thy faith, be it unto thee even as thou wilt.

From the Gospel.

I WILL not let Thee go; Thou Help in time
of need!
Heap ill on ill
I trust Thee still,
E'en when it seems that thou wouldst slay indeed!
Do as Thou wilt with me,
I yet will cling to Thee,
Hide Thou Thy face, yet, Help in time of need,
I will not let Thee go!

I WILL not let Thee go; should I forsake my bliss?
No, Lord, Thou'rt mine,
And I am Thine,
Thee will I hold when all things else I miss.
Though dark and sad the night,
Joy cometh with Thy light,
O Thou my Sun; should I forsake my bliss?
I will not let Thee go!

I WILL not let Thee go, my God, my Life, my Lord!
Not Death can tear
Me from His care,
Who for my sake His soul in death outpour'd.
Thou diedst for love to me,
I say in love to Thee,
E'en when my heart shall break, my God, my Life,
my Lord,
I will not let Thee go!

DESZLER. 1692.

64

Third Sunday in Lent

Awake, thou that sleepest, and arise from the dead, and Christ shall give thee light.—From the Epistle.

AWAKE, O man, and from thee shake
    This heavy sleep of sin!
Soon shall the Highest vengeance take,
    Soon shall His wrath begin

To smite the wretched sinner home;
In awful terrors He shall come,
To mete to all on earth their due reward,
Only the righteous spares our angry Lord.

Come then, ye sinners, great and small,
Weeping and mourning sore,
Low down before His footstool fall,
And vow to sin no more.
In faith and godliness array
Your souls against that final day,
So shall ye 'scape His wrath, and blessed die,
Heirs of the kingdom with your Lord on high.

Oh lay to heart this wondrous thought,
Through what sore agony
And death was your redemption bought,
And to your Saviour flee
Ere yet too late; the world disown,
And fix your love on Christ alone,
And do His will; for at the final doom,
Those who dishonour'd Him shall wrath consume.

Turn Thou us, and we shall be turn'd;
Thou broughtest back of old
Thy straying people, when they yearn'd
After their proper fold :
Even so forgive what we have done.
Accept us in Thy blessed Son,
And let Thy Holy Spirit be our guide,
That we may spread Thy praises far and wide!

CRASSELIUS. 1697.

Fourth Sunday in Lent.

Grant, we beseech Thee, Almighty God, that we, who for our evil deeds do worthily deserve to be punished, by the comfort of Thy grace may mercifully be relieved; through our Lord and Saviour, Jesus Christ.

From the Collect.

HERE, O my God, I cast me at Thy feet,
Ready to suffer what Thou thinkest meet ;
Yet look on me, great God, with pitying eyes,
Reward me not for mine iniquities !

Too oft, alas ! my heart hath loved to stray
Downward along Sin's broad and easy way ;
And worldly pride and carnal lusts most foul
Were shameless cherish'd in my inmost soul.

Thy Majesty have I offended, Lord,
And set at nought Thy law, Thy holy Word ;
I had not learnt Thy righteous wrath to dread,
Nor saw the vengeance gathering o'er my head.

O wretched man, what evil have I wrought !
Now in the snares of Sin a captive caught,
I learn, O Sin, how fell and keen thy smart !
O wrath of God, how terrible thou art !

Is there no way, can I no helper find,
Who may these heavy chains of sin unbind !
Can man nor creature show me any place,
Where I may flee and hide me from God's face !

Nay, I must flee to God Himself, from whom
Our life and help, our hope and safety come;
What all the world must unaccomplish'd leave,
Thou, for Thou art Almighty, canst achieve.

Think on the covenant Thou hast never broken,
Think on the steadfast oath Thyself hast spoken;
Know that I am a God, Thy promise saith,
Who hath no pleasure in a sinner's death.

Then let the arms of love be round me thrown,
Have pity on me, hear my bitter moan,
Call back Thy sheep, that wandering far astray,
Was lost in sin, nor knew its homeward way.

Grant me to rule my inner life aright,
And act and speak as ever in Thy sight,
A friend to all true virtue, but a foe
To all Thou hatest, sins and follies low.

Thou Merciful! what thanks and praise shall be
For Thy great goodness offer'd unto Thee,
As is most meet, while here my days I spend,
And yonder in the world that shall not end!

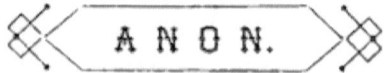

ANON.

FIFTH SUNDAY IN LENT.

Out of the depths have I called unto Thee, O Lord; Lord, hear my voice. If Thou, Lord, wilt be extreme to mark what is done amiss, O Lord, who may abide it?—Ps. cxxx. 1, 3.

UT of the depths I cry to Thee,
　　Lord God! oh hear my prayer!
Incline a gracious ear to me,
　　And bid me not despair:
If Thou rememberest each misdeed,
If each should have its rightful meed,
　　Lord, who shall stand before Thee?

'Tis through Thy love alone we gain
　　The pardon of our sin;
The strictest life is but in vain,
　　Our works can nothing win,
That none should boast himself of aught,
But own in fear Thy grace hath wrought
　　What in him seemeth righteous.

Wherefore my hope is in the Lord,
　My works I count but dust,
I build not there, but on His word,
　And in His goodness trust.
Up to His care myself I yield,
He is my tower, my rock, my shield,
　　And for His help I tarry.

And though it linger till the night,
　And round again to morn,
My heart shall ne'er mistrust Thy might,
　Nor count itself forlorn.
Do thus, O ye of Israel's seed,
Ye of the Spirit born indeed,
　　Wait for your God's appearing.

Though great our sins and sore our wounds,
　And deep and dark our fall,
His helping mercy hath no bounds,
　His love surpasseth all.
Our trusty loving Shepherd He,
Who shall at last set Israel free
　　From all their sin and sorrow.

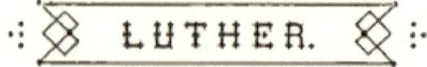

∴ ⊗ LUTHER. ⊗ ⋮

1524.

*And the multitudes that went before, and that followed, cried, saying,
Hosanna to the Son of David; Blessed is He that cometh in the name
of the Lord; Hosanna in the highest.* Matt. xxi. 9.

HOSANNA to the Son of David! Raise
    Triumphal arches to His praise,
      For Him prepare a throne
    Who comes at last to Zion—to His own!
  Strew palms around, make plain and straight the way
For Him who His triumphal entry holds to-day!

Hosanna! Welcome above all Thou art!
  Make ready each to lay his heart
    Low down before His feet!
  Come, let us hasten forth our Lord to meet,
And bid Him enter in at Zion's gates,
Where thousand-voiced welcome on His coming waits.

Hosanna! Prince of Peace and Lord of Might!
  We hail Thee Conqueror in the fight!
    All Thou with toil hast won,
  Shall be our booty when the battle's done.
Thy right hand ever hath the rule and sway,
Thy kingdom standeth fast when all things else decay.

Hosanna! best-beloved and noble Guest!
  Who makest us by Thy behest
    Heirs of Thy realm with Thee.
  Oh let us therefore never weary be
To stand and serve before Thy righteous throne,
We know no king but Thee, rule Thou o'er us alone!

Hosanna! Come, the time draws on apace,
  We long Thy mercy to embrace;
    This servant's form can ne'er
  Conceal the majesty Thy acts declare:
Too well art Thou here in Thy Zion known,
Who art the Son of God, and yet art David's Son.

Hosanna! Lord, be Thou our help and friend,
Thy aid to us in mercy send,
That each may bring his soul
An offering unto Thee, unstain'd and whole.
Thou wilt have none for Thy disciples, Lord,
But those who truly keep, not only hear Thy word.

Hosanna! Let us in Thy footsteps tread,
Nor that sad Mount of Olives dread
Where we must weep and watch,
Until the far-off song of joy we catch
From Heaven our Bethphage, where we shall sing
Hosanna in the highest to our God and King!

Hosanna! Let us sound it far and wide!
Enter Thou in and here abide,
Thou Blessed of the Lord!
Why standest Thou without, why roam'st abroad?
Hosanna! Make Thy home with us for ever!
Thou comest, Lord! and nought us from Thy love shall
sever.
Hallelujah.

SCHMOLCK.

1704.

AND WHEN HE WAS COME NEAR, HE BEHELD THE CITY AND WEPT OVER IT
LUKE. XIX. 14.

MONDAY IN PASSION WEEK.

HOU weepest o'er Jerusalem,
Lord Jesus, bitter tears;
But deepest comfort lies in them
For us, whose sins have fill'd our souls with fears:
Since that they tell,
When sinners turn to Thee Thou lov'st it well,
And surely wilt efface, of Thy unbounded grace,
All the misdeeds that on our conscience dwell.

When God's just wrath and anger burn
  Against me for my sin,
To these sad tears of Thine I turn,
  And watching them fresh hope and courage win;
    For God doth prize
These drops so greatly, that before His eyes
Who sprinkles o'er his soul with them is clean and whole,
And from his sorrows' depth new joy shall rise.

Earth is the home of tears and woe,
  Where we must often weep,
Fighting the world our mighty foe,
  Whose enmity to Thee doth never sleep;
    My heart is torn
Afresh each day by her fierce rage and scorn,
But in my saddest hours, I think upon those showers
That tell how Thou hast all our sorrows borne.

Thou countest up my tears and sighs,
  E'en were they numberless;
Not one is hidden from Thine eyes,
  Thou ne'er forgettest me in my distress,
    But when they rain
Before Thee, Thou dost quickly turn again,
Hast pity on my woe, and makest me to know
What sweetest joy lies hid in sorest pain.

We sow in tears; but let us keep
  Our faith in God, and trust Him still,
Yonder our harvest we shall reap,
  Where gladness every heart and voice shall fill.

Such joy is there
No mortal tongue its glory can declare,
A joy that shall endure, unchanging deep and pure,
That shall be ours, if here the cross we bear.

O Christ, I thank Thee for Thy tears;
Those tears have won for me
That I shall wear, through endless years,
A crown of joy before my God and Thee.
All weeping o'er,
Up to Thy chosen saints I once shall soar,
And there Thy pity praise, in more befitting lays,
Thou Glory of Thy Church, for evermore.

HEERMANN.
1630.

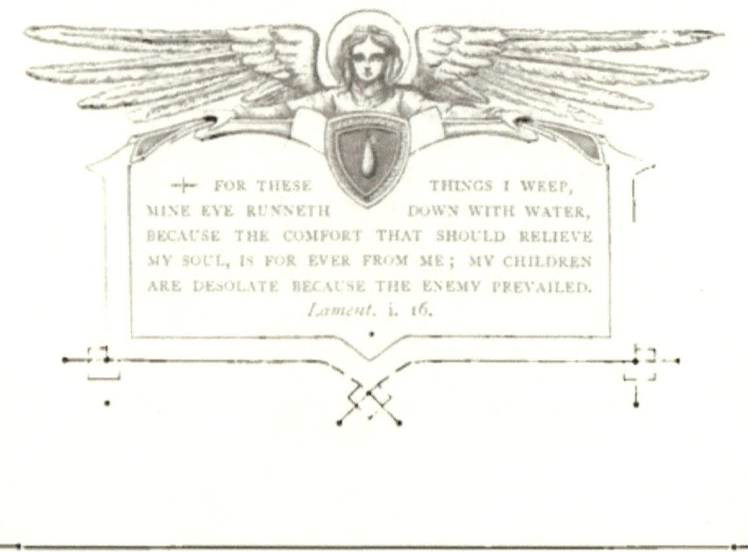

FOR THESE THINGS I WEEP,
MINE EYE RUNNETH DOWN WITH WATER,
BECAUSE THE COMFORT THAT SHOULD RELIEVE
MY SOUL, IS FOR EVER FROM ME; MY CHILDREN
ARE DESOLATE BECAUSE THE ENEMY PREVAILED.
Lament. i. 16.

Tuesday in Passion Week.

*By the which will we are sanctified, through the offering of the
body of Jesus Christ once for all.*

Heb. x. 10.

LORD! Thy death and passion give
　　Strength and comfort at my need,
　　Every hour while here I live
　　On Thy love my soul shall feed.
Doth some evil thought upstart?
Lo, Thy cross defends my heart.
Shows the peril, and I shrink
Back from loitering on the brink.

Doth my carnal nature yearn
　　After wanton joys? again
Quickly to Thy cross I turn,
　　And her voice is heard in vain.
Cometh strong temptation's hour,
When my foe puts forth his power?
Shelter'd by this holy shield,
Soon I drive him from the field.

Would the world my steps entice
　　To yon wide and level road,
Fill'd with mirth and pleasant vice?
　　Lord, I think upon the load
Thou didst once for me endure,
And I fly all thoughts impure:
Thinking on Thy bitter pains,
Hush'd in prayer my heart remains.

Yes, Thy cross hath power to heal
  All the wounds of sin and strife,
Lost in Thee my heart doth feel
  Sudden warmth and nobler life.
In my saddest, darkest grief,
Let Thy sweetness bring relief,
Thou who camest but to save,
Thou who fearedst not the grave!

Lord, in Thee I place my trust,
  Thou art my defence and tower;
Death Thou treadest in the dust,
  O'er my soul he hath no power.
That I may have part in Thee,
Help and save and comfort me,
Give me of Thy grace and might,
Resurrection, life and light.

Fount of Good, within me dwell,
  For the peace Thy presence sheds
Keeps us safe in conflict fell,
  Charms the pain from dying beds.
Hide me close within Thine arm,
Where no foe can hurt or harm;
Whoso, Lord, in Thee doth rest,
He hath conquer'd, he is blest.

HEERMANN.

1644.

Wednesday in Passion Week.

Now once in the end of the world hath He appeared, to put away sin by the sacrifice of Himself.

From the Epistle.

When sorrow and remorse
Prey at my heart, to Thee
I look, who on the holy cross
Wast slain for me.
Ah Lord, Thy precious blood was spilt
For me, O most unworthy,
To take away my guilt.

Oh wonder past belief!
Behold the Master spares
His servants, and sore pain and grief
For them He bears.
God stoopeth from His throne on high,
For me His guilty creature,
He deigns as man to die.

Though countless were the sins
That weigh'd me to the dust,
Christ's death for me the favour wins
Of God most just.
His precious blood my debts hath paid,
Of hell and all its torments
I am no more afraid.

My heart is fill'd with ruth,
Thinking on all Thou'st borne,
How mighty love and tender truth
Were crown'd with thorn.
In songs of thanks I'll spend my breath
For Thy sad cry, Thy sufferings,
Thy wrongs, Thy guiltless death.

Thy Passion, Lord, inspires
My spirit day by day,
With strength from all low dark desires
To flee away.
This thought I fain would cherish most,
What pain my soul's redemption
To Thee, O Saviour, cost.

Whate'er the burden be,
The cross upon me laid,
Or want or shame, I look to Thee,
Be Thou mine aid.
Give patience, give me strength to take
Thee for my bright example,
And all the world forsake.

Let me to others do,
As Thou hast done to me,
Love them with love unfeign'd and true,
Their servant be
Of willing heart, nor seek my own,
But as Thou, Lord, hast helped us,
From purest love alone.

And let Thy sorrows cheer
My soul when I depart ;
Give strength to cast away all fear,
And tell my heart
That since my trust is in Thy grace,
Thou wilt accept me yonder,
Where I shall see Thy face.

GESENIUS. 1646.

INRI · SPQR

HE · WASHED · HIS · HANDS · BEFORE · THE · MVLTITVDE · SAYING · I · AM · INNOCENT · OF · THE · DEATH · OF · THIS · IVST · PERSON · SEE · YE

THVRSDAY · IN · PASSION · WEEK

Pilate therefore, willing to release Jesus, spake again to them. But they cried saying, Crucify Him, crucify Him. And he said unto them the third time, Why, what evil hath He done?

From the Gospel.

ALAS, dear Lord, what evil hast Thou done,
That such sharp sentence from Thy judge hath won!
What are His crimes, and what the guilt, oh, tell
Wherein He fell!

They scourge Him, crown Him with a crown of thorn,
They smite His face with bitter mock and scorn,
They give Him gall to drink, they pierce His side,
The Crucified!

From head to foot was there no spot in me
Unscarr'd by sin, from taint of evil free;
My sins had weigh'd me down that I should dwell
For aye in Hell.

Whence come these sorrows, whence this cruel woe?
It was my sins that struck the fatal blow;
Mine were the wrath and anguish, dearest Lord,
    On Thee outpour'd.

What strangest punishment! The Shepherd good
For erring sheep here pours His own heart's blood,
The servants' debts are on the Master laid,
    Who all hath paid.

Oh wondrous love, love that no measure knows,
That brought Thee, Christ, to drink this cup of woes!
Full of the world's vain joys and hopes was I,
    While Thou must die!

O mighty King! mighty beyond all time!
Fain would I sound Thy praise through every clime!
A gift were meet for Thee, my anxious thought
    Long time hath sought.

But human wisdom searches, Lord, in vain
To find aught like Thy pity, or Thy pain.
How shall my works, though toiling day and night,
    Thy love requite?

Yet have I somewhat that my Lord can please;
I can renounce sweet sins and selfish ease,
And quench the unhallow'd fires that back would lure
    To thoughts impure.

But since my strength, alas, will ne'er prevail
My strong desires upon the cross to nail,
Oh let Thy Spirit rule my heart, who leads
      To all good deeds.

Then shall Thy mercy fill my every thought,
I love Thee so, the world to me is nought ;
My sole endeavour, Lord, is to fulfil
      Thy holy will.

My all I risk to magnify Thy name,
No cross shall daunt me, no reproach or shame ;
Man's fiercest threats I will not lay to heart,
      Nor Death's worst smart.

In truth my sacrifice is nothing worth,
Yet Thou in mercy wilt not cast it forth ;
Thou'lt put me not to shame, but for love's sake
      My offering take.

Lord Jesus, once on high amongst Thine own,
Shall I stand crown'd with light before Thy throne !
Where sweetest hymns are ever ringing round,
      My voice shall sound.

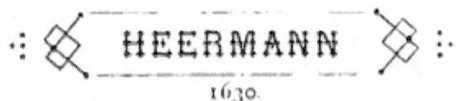

HEERMANN

1630.

Good Friday.

MORNING.

*He was wounded for our transgres-
sions, He was bruised for our
iniquities; the chastisement of
our peace was upon Him, and
with His stripes we are healed.*

From the Lesson.

Ah wounded Head! Must Thou
    Endure such shame and scorn!
The blood is trickling from Thy brow
    Pierced by the crown of thorn.
    Thou who wast crown'd on high
    With light and majesty,
In deep dishonour here must die,
    Yet here I welcome Thee!

    Thou noble countenance!
    All earthly lights are pale
Before the brightness of that glance,
    At which a world shall quail.
    How is it quenched and gone!
    Those gracious eyes how dim!
Whence grew that cheek so pale and wan?
    Who dared to scoff at Him?

All lovely hues of life,
    That glow'd on lip and cheek,
Have vanish'd in that awful strife;
    The Mighty One is weak.
    Pale Death has won the day,
    He triumphs in this hour
When Strength and Beauty fade away,
    And yield them to his power.

    Ah Lord, Thy woes belong,
    Thy cruel pains, to me,
The burden of my sin and wrong
    Hath all been laid on Thee.
    Behold me where I kneel,
    Wrath were my rightful lot,
One glance of love yet let me feel!
    Redeemer, spurn me not!

    My Guardian, own me Thine;
    My Shepherd, bear me home:
O Fount of mercy, Source Divine,
    From Thee what blessings come!
    How oft Thy mouth has fed
    My soul with angels' food,
How oft Thy Spirit o'er me shed
    His stores of heavenly good!

    Ah would that 1 could share
    Thy cross, Thy bitter woes!
All true delight lies hidden there,
    Thence all true comfort flows.

LYRA GERMANICA.

Ah well were it for me
That I could end my strife,
And die upon the cross with Thee,
Who art my Life of life!

My soul is all o'erfraught,
O Jesus, dearest Friend,
With thankful love to Him who sought
Such woe for such an end.
Grant me as true a faith,
As Thou art true to me,
That so the icy sleep of death
Be but a rest in Thee.

Yes, when I must depart,
Depart Thou not from me;
When Death is creeping to my heart,
Bear Thou mine agony.
When faith and courage sink,
O'erwhelm'd with dread dismay,
Come Thou who ne'er from pain didst shrink,
And chase my fears away.

Come to me ere I die,
My comfort and my shield;
Then gazing on Thy cross can I
Calmly my spirit yield.
On Thee, when life is past,
My darkening eyes shall dwell,
My heart in faith shall hold Thee fast;
Who dieth thus, dies well.

PAUL GERHARDT. 1659.

GOOD FRIDAY.

EVENING.

But God commendeth His love toward us, in that, while we were yet sinners, Christ died for us.

Rom. v. 8.

THOU Holiest Love, whom most I love,
   Who art my long'd-for only bliss,
   Whom tenderest pity erst did move
   To fathom woe and death's abyss
Who once didst suffer for my good,
   And die my guilty debts to pay,
Thou Lamb of God, whose precious blood
   Can take a world's misdeeds away;

Thou Love, who didst such anguish bear
   Upon the Mount of agony,
And yet with ceaseless watchful care
   Dost yearn o'er us so tenderly;
Thou camest not Thy will to seek,
   But all Thy Father's will obey,
Bearing the cross in patience meek,
   That Thou might'st take our curse away.

O Love, who with unflinching heart
   Enduredst all disgrace and shame;
O Love, who mid the keenest smart
   Of dying pangs wert still the same:

Who didst Thy changeless virtue prove
   E'en with Thy latest parting breath,
And spakest words of gentlest love
   When soul and body sank in death ;

O Love, through sorrows manifold
   Hast Thou betroth'd me as a bride,
By ceaseless gifts, by love untold,
   Hast bound me ever to Thy side ;
Oh let the weary ache, the smart,
   Of life's long tale of pain and loss,
Be gently still'd within my heart
   At thought of Thee, and of Thy cross !

O Love, who dying thus for me,
   Hast won me an eternal good
Through sorest anguish on the tree,
   I ever think upon Thy blood ;
I ever thank Thy sacred wounds,
   Thou wounded Love, Thou Holiest,
But most when life is near its bounds,
   And in Thy bosom safe I rest.

O Love, who unto death hast grieved
   For this cold heart, unworthy Thine,
Whom once the chill dark grave received,
   I thank Thee for that grief divine ;
I give Thee thanks that Thou didst die
   To win eternal life for me,
To bring salvation from on high ;
   Oh draw me up through love to Thee !

                ANGELUS. 1657.

EASTER EVEN.

And Joseph wrapped the body in a clean linen cloth, and laid it in his own new tomb, which he had hewn out in the rock.

From the Gospel.

REST of the weary! Thou
    Thyself art resting now,
Where lowly in Thy sepulchre Thou liest :
    From out her deathly sleep
    My soul doth start, to weep
So sad a wonder, that Thou Saviour diest !

    Thy bitter anguish o'er,
    To this dark tomb they bore
Thee, Life of Life—Thee, Lord of all creation !
    The hollow rocky cave
    Must serve Thee for a grave,
Who wast Thyself the Rock of our Salvation !

    O Prince of Life ! I know
    That when I too lie low,
Thou wilt at last my soul from death awaken ;
    And thus I will not shrink
    From the grave's awful brink ;
The heart that trusts in Thee shall ne'er be shaken.

    To me the darksome tomb
    Is but a narrow room,
Where I may rest in peace from sorrow free ;
    Thy death shall give me power
    To cry in that dark hour,
O Death, O Grave, where is your victory !

    The grave can nought destroy,
    Only the flesh can die,
And e'en the body triumphs o'er decay :

Clothed by Thy wondrous might
In robes of dazzling light,
This flesh shall burst the grave at that last Day.

My Jesus, day by day,
Help me to watch and pray,
Beside the tomb where in my heart Thou'rt laid.
Thy bitter death shall be
My constant memory,
My guide at last into Death's awful shade.

S. FRANCK. 1711.

EASTER DAY.

MORNING.

*Christ being raised from the dead dieth no more:
death hath no more dominion over Him.*

From the Anthem.

THE bonds of Death He lay,
  Who for our offence was slain,
But the Lord is risen to-day,
  Christ hath brought us life again.
Wherefore let us all rejoice,
Singing loud with cheerful voice
            Hallelujah !

Of the sons of men was none
  Who could break the bonds of Death,
Sin this mischief dire had done,
  Innocent was none on earth ;
Wherefore Death grew strong and bold,
Death would all men captive hold.
            Hallelujah !

Jesus Christ, God's only Son,
  Came at last our foe to smite,
All our sins away hath done,
  Done away Death's power and right,
Only the form of Death is left,
Of his sting he is bereft ;
            Hallelujah.

'Twas a wondrous war, I trow,
　　When Life and Death together fought;
But life hath triumph'd o'er his foe,
　　Death is mock'd and set at nought;
Yea, 'tis as the Scripture saith,
Christ through death has conquer'd Death.
　　　　　　　Hallelujah.

Now our Paschal Lamb is He,
　　And by Him alone we live,
Who to death upon the tree,
　　For our sake Himself did give.
Faith His blood strikes on our door,
Death dares never harm us more.
　　　　　　　Hallelujah.

On this day most blest of days,
　　Let us keep high festival,
For our God hath show'd His grace,
　　And our Sun hath risen on all,
And our hearts rejoice to see
Sin and night before Him flee.
　　　　　　　Hallelujah.

To the supper of the Lord,
　　Gladly will we come to-day,
The word of peace is now restored,
　　The old leaven is put away;
Christ will be our food alone,
Faith no life but His doth own.
　　　　　　　Hallelujah.

　　　　　　　　　LUTHER. 1524.

EASTER DAY.

EVENING.

If ye then be risen with Christ, seek those things which
are above, where Christ sitteth on the right hand of God.

From the Epistle.

GLORIOUS Head, Thou livest now!
Let us Thy members share Thy life;
Canst Thou behold their need, nor bow
To raise Thy children from the strife
With self and sin, with death and dark distress,
That they may live to Thee in holiness?

Earth knows Thee not, but evermore
Thou liv'st in Paradise, in peace;
Oh fain my soul would thither soar,
Oh let me from the creatures cease:
Dead to the world, but to Thy Spirit known,
I live to Thee, O Prince of life, alone.

Break through my bonds whate'er it cost,
What is not Thine within me slay,
Give me the lot I covet most,
To rise as Thou hast risen to-day.
I nought can do, a slave to death I pine,
Work Thou in me, O Power and Life Divine!

Work Thou in me, and heavenward guide
My thoughts and wishes, that my heart
Waver no more nor turn aside,
But fix for ever where Thou art.
Thou art not far from us; who loves Thee well,
While yet on earth in heaven with Thee may dwell.

TERSTEEGEN. 1731.

93

Monday in Easter Week.

And they told what things were done in the way, and how He was known to them in breaking of bread. And as they thus spake, Jesus Himself stood in the midst of them, and saith unto them, Peace be unto you.

From the Gospel.

WELCOME Thou victor in the strife,
  Now welcome from the cave!
To-day we triumph in Thy life
  Around Thine empty grave.

Our enemy is put to shame,
  His short-lived triumph o'er;
Our God is with us, we exclaim,
  We fear our foe no more.

The dwellings of the just resound
  With songs of victory;
For in their midst, Lord, Thou art found,
  And bringest peace with Thee.

O share with us the spoils, we pray,
  Thou diedst to achieve;
We meet within Thy house to-day
  Our portion to receive:

And let Thy conquering banner wave
  O'er hearts Thou makest free,
And point the path that from the grave
  Leads heavenward up to Thee.

We bury all our sin and crime
   Deep in our Saviour's tomb,
And seek the treasure there, that time
   Nor change can e'er consume.

We die with Thee; oh let us live
   Henceforth to Thee aright;
The blessings Thou hast died to give,
   Be daily in our sight.

Fearless we lay us in the tomb,
   And sleep the night away,
If Thou art there to break the gloom,
   And call us back to day.

Death hurts us not; his power is gone,
   And pointless all his darts;
Now hath God's favour on us shone,
   And joy fills all our hearts.

SCHMOLK

Tuesday in Easter Week

I KNOW that my
Redeemer liveth ..
and though after my
skin, worms destroy
this body, yet in my
flesh shall I see God.
Job xix. 25, 26.

FOR this corruptible
must put on in-
corruption, and this
mortal must put on
immortality.

From the
Lesson.

Jesus my Redeemer lives,
  Christ my trust is dead no more;
In the strength this knowledge gives
  Shall not all my fears be o'er,
Though the night of Death be fraught
Still with many an anxious thought !

Jesus my Redeemer lives,
  And His life I once shall see;
Bright the hope this promise gives,
  Where He is I too shall be.
Shall I fear then ? Can the Head
Rise and leave the members dead ?

Close to Him my soul is bound
  In the bonds of Hope enclasp'd;
Faith's strong hand this hold hath found,
  And the Rock hath firmly grasp'd :
And no ban of death can part
From our Lord the trusting heart.

I shall see Him with these eyes,
  Him whom I shall surely know;
Not another shall I rise,
  With His love this heart shall glow :
Only there shall disappear
Weakness in and round me here.

Ye who suffer, sigh, and moan,
  Fresh and glorious there shall reign ;
Earthly here the seed is sown,

Heavenly it shall rise again ;
Natural here the death we die,
Spiritual our life on high.

Body, be thou of good cheer,
  In thy Saviour's care rejoice,
Give not place to gloom and fear,
  Dead, thou yet shalt know His voice,
When the final trump is heard,
And the deaf cold grave is stirr'd.

Laugh to scorn then death and hell,
  Laugh to scorn the gloomy grave ;
Caught into the air to dwell
  With the Lord who comes to save,
We shall trample on our foes,
Mortal weakness, fear and woes.

Only see ye that your heart
  Rise betimes from earthly lust ;
Would ye there with Him have part,
  Here obey your Lord and trust,
Fix your hearts beyond the skies,
Whither ye yourselves would rise.

LOUISA HENRIETTA,

ELECTRESS OF BRANDENBURGH.

1653.

First Sunday after Easter.

God hath given to us eternal life, and this life is in His Son.

From the Epistle.

HAT had I been if Thou wert not?
    What were I now if Thou wert gone?
Ah, fear and anguish were my lot,
    In this wide world I stood alone;
Whate'er I loved were safe no more,
    The future were a dark abyss;
To whom could I my sorrows pour,
    If Thee my laden heart should miss?

Longing for love through lonely years,
    The gloom of night came o'er my day;
I follow'd, yet with secret tears,
    The world's wild joys, and own'd her sway;
Till restless from her turmoil driven,
    I turn'd within,—and grief was there:
Ah, had we not a Friend in heaven,
    Who, who his lot on earth could bear!

But when Thou mak'st Thy presence felt,
    And when the soul hath grasp'd Thee right,
How fast the dreary shadows melt
    Beneath Thy warm and living light!

In Thee I find a nobler birth,
    A glory o'er the world I see,
And Paradise returns to earth,
    And blooms again for us in Thee.

Thou strong and loving Son of Man,
  Redeemer from the bonds of sin,
'Tis Thou the living spark dost fan
  That sets my heart on fire within.
Thou openest heaven once more to men,
  The soul's true home, Thy Kingdom, Lord,
And I can trust and hope again,
  And feel myself akin to God.

Brethren, go forth beside all ways,
  The wanderer greet with outstretch'd hand,
And call him back who darkly strays,
  And bid him join our gladsome band.
That Heaven hath stoop'd to earth below,
  Proclaim the glad news everywhere,
That all may learn our faith, and know
  They too may find an entrance there.

AFTER

· NOVALIS. ·

ABOUT

1795.

Second Sunday After Easter.

Jesus said, I am the Good Shepherd; the Good Shepherd giveth His life for His sheep.

From the Gospel.

LOVING Shepherd, kind and true,
Wilt Thou not in pity come
To Thy Lamb? As shepherds do,
Bear me in Thy bosom home;
Take me hence from earth's annoy
To Thy home of endless joy.

See how I have gone astray
In this earthly wilderness;
Come and take me soon away
To Thy flock who dwell in bliss,
And Thy glory, Lord, behold,
Safe within Thy heavenly fold.

For I fain would gaze on Thee,
   With the lambs to whom 'tis given
That they feed, from danger free,
   In the happy fields of heaven ;
Praising Thee, all terrors o'er,
Never can they wander more.

Here I live in sore distress,
   Fearing, watching, hour by hour ;
For my foes around me press,
   And I know their craft and power :
Lord, Thy lamb can never be
Safe one moment, but with Thee.

O Lord Jesus, let me not
   'Mid the ravening wolves e'er fall,
Help me as a shepherd ought,
   That I may escape them all :
Bear me homeward in Thy breast,
To Thy fold of endless rest.

· ANGELUS. ·

1657.

Third Sunday After Easter

And ye now therefore have sorrow; but I will see you again, and your heart shall rejoice, and your joy no man taketh from you.

From the Gospel.

COMETH sunshine after rain,
After mourning joy again,
After heavy bitter grief
Dawneth surely sweet relief!
And my soul, who from her height
Sank to realms of woe and night,
Wingeth now to heaven her flight.

He whom this world dares not face
Hath refresh'd me with His grace.
And His mighty hand unbound
Chains of hell about me wound;

Quicker, stronger, leaps my blood,
Since His mercy, like a flood,
Pour'd o'er all my heart for good.

Bitter anguish have I borne,
Keen regret my heart hath torn,
Sorrow dimm'd my weeping eyes,
Satan blinded me with lies;
    Yet at last am I set free,
    Help, protection, love, to me
    Once more true companions be.

None was ever left a prey,
None was ever turn'd away,
Who had given himself to God,
And on Him had cast his load.
    Who in God his hope hath placed
    Shall not life in pain outwaste,
    Fullest joy he yet shall taste.

Though to-day may not fulfil
All thy hopes, have patience still,
For perchance to-morrow's sun
Sees thy happier days begun;
    As God willeth march the hours,
    Bringing joy at last in showers,
    When whate'er we ask'd is ours.

Once a pain that would not cease
Gnaw'd my heart without release,
Sorrow bow'd me 'neath her yoke,
Then in sadness oft I spoke:

Now no hope is left for me,
And no rest, until I be
Whelm'd beneath Death's sunless sea.

But when I was worn with care,
Fill'd with dread well-nigh despair;
When with watching many a night,
On me fell pale sickness' blight;
    When my courage fail'd me fast,
    Camest Thou, my God, at last,
    And my woes were quickly past.

Yea, Thou God didst make an end,
Thou such help and strength didst send,
That I nevermore can praise
As I ought, Thy matchless grace;
    When I sought with anxious fear,
    And could see no refuge here,
    Lo! I found Thy help was near.

Now as long as here I roam,
On this earth have house and home,
Shall this wondrous gleam from Thee
Shine through all my memory.
    To my God I yet will cling.
    All my life the praises sing
    That from thankful hearts outspring.

Every sorrow, every smart,
That the Eternal Father's heart
Hath appointed me of yore,
Or hath yet for me in store,

As my life flows on I'll take
Calmly, gladly for His sake,
No more faithless murmurs make.

I will meet distress and pain
I will greet e'en Death's dark reign,
I will lay me in the grave,
With a heart still glad and brave;
    Whom the Strongest doth defend,
    Whom the Highest counts His friend,
    Cannot perish in the end.

PAUL GERHARDT.

1659.

FOR
I KNOW THAT
MY REDEEMER LIVETH,
AND THAT HE SHALL STAND
AT THE LATTER DAY UPON THE EARTH:
AND THOUGH AFTER MY SKIN WORMS DESTROY
THIS BODY, YET IN MY FLESH SHALL I SEE GOD
Job xix. 25, 26.

Fourth Sunday after Easter.

It is expedient for you that I go away, for
if I go not away, the Comforter
will not come unto you.

From the Gospel.

HOLY Ghost! my Comforter!
Now from highest heaven appear,
Shed Thy gracious radiance here.

Come to them who suffer dearth,
With Thy gifts of priceless worth,
Lighten all who dwell on earth!

Thou the heart's most precious guest,
Thou of comforters the best,
Give to us, the o'er-laden, rest.

Come, in Thee our toil is sweet,
Shelter from the noon-day heat,
From whom sorrow flieth fleet.

Blessed Sun of Grace! O'er all
Faithful hearts who on Thee call,
Let Thy joy and solace fall.

What without Thy aid is wrought,
Skilful deed or wisest thought,
God will count but vain and nought.

Cleanse us, Lord, from sinful stain,
O'er the parchèd heart oh rain,
Heal the wounded from its pain.

Bend the stubborn will to Thine,
Melt the cold with fire divine,
Erring hearts aright incline.

Grant us, Lord, who cry to Thee,
Steadfast in the faith to be,
Give Thy gifts of charity.

May we live in holiness,
And in death find happiness,
And abide with Thee in bliss!

TRANSLATION OF THE 17TH CENTURY AFTER

KING ROBERT OF FRANCE.

ABOUT A. D.

1000.

FIFTH SUNDAY
AFTER EASTER.

These things have I spoken unto you, that in me ye might have peace.
In the world ye shall have tribulation; but be of good
cheer, I have overcome the world.

From the Gospel.

hrist Thou the champion of that war-
worn host
Who bear Thy cross, haste, help, or we
are lost;
The schemes of those who long our blood
have sought
Bring Thou to nought.

Do Thou Thyself for us Thy children fight,
Withstand the devil, quell his rage and might,
Whate'er assails Thy members left below
Do Thou o'erthrow:

And give us peace; peace in the church and school,
Peace to the powers who o'er our country rule,
Peace to the conscience, peace within the heart,
Do Thou impart.

So shall Thy goodness here be still adored,
Thou guardian of Thy little flock, dear Lord,
And heaven and earth through all eternity
Shall worship Thee.

LÖWENSTERN.
During the Thirty Years' War.

ASCENSION DAY.

This same Jesus which is taken up from you into heaven, shall so come,
in like manner as ye have seen Him go into heaven.

From the Epistle.

LORD, on earth I dwell in pain;
    Here in anguish I must lie:
Wherefore leav'st Thou me again,
    Why ascendest Thou on high?
Take me, take me hence with Thee,
Or abide, Lord, still in me;
Let Thy love and gifts be left,
That I be not all bereft.

Leave Thy heart with me behind,
  Take mine hence with Thee away;
Let my sighs an entrance find
  To Thy heaven whene'er I pray.
When I cannot pray, oh plead
With Thy Father in my stead;
Seated now at God's right hand,
Help us here Thy faithful band.

Help me earthly toys to spurn,
  Raise my thoughts from things below;
Mortal am I, yet I yearn
  Heavenly like my Lord to grow,
That my time through faith may be
Order'd for eternity;
Till we rise, all perils o'er,
Whither Thou hast gone before.

In due season come again,
  As was promised us of old;
Raise the members that have lain
  Gnaw'd of death beneath the mould.
Judge the evil world that deems
Thy sure words but empty dreams;
Then for all our sorrows past,
Let us know Thy joy at last.

NEUMANN.

1700.

SUNDAY AFTER ASCENSION DAY.

These all confessed that they were strangers and pilgrims on the earth. . . . For they desired a better country, that is, an heavenly ; wherefore God is not ashamed to be called their God; for He hath prepared for them a city.

Heb. xi. 13, 16.

EAVENWARD doth our journey tend,
 We are strangers here on earth,
Through the wilderness we wend
 Towards the Canaan of our birth.
Here we roam a pilgrim band,
Yonder is our native land.

Heavenward stretch, my soul, thy wings,
 Heavenly nature canst thou claim,
There is nought of earthly things
 Worthy to be all thine aim ;
Every soul that God inspires
Back to Him, its Source, aspires.

Heavenward ! doth His Spirit cry,
 When I hear Him in His Word,
Showing thus the rest on high,
 Where I shall be with my Lord :
When His Word fills all my thought,
Oft to heaven my soul is caught.

Heavenward ever would I haste,
    When Thy table, Lord, is spread;
Heavenly strength on earth I taste,

Feeding on the Living Bread ;
Such is e'en on earth our fare,
Who Thy marriage feast shall share.

Heavenward ! Faith discerns the prize
   That is waiting us afar,
And my heart would swiftly rise,
   High o'er sun and moon and star,
To that Light behind the veil
Where all earthly splendours pale.

Heavenward Death shall lead at last,
   To the home where I would be,
All my sorrows overpast,
   I shall triumph there with Thee,
Jesus, who hast gone before,
That we too might Heavenward soar.

Heavenward ! Heavenward ! Only this
   Is my watchword on the earth ;
For the love of heavenly bliss
   Counting all things little worth.
Heavenward all my being tends,
Till in Heaven my journey ends.

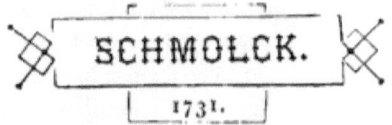

SCHMOLCK.

1731.

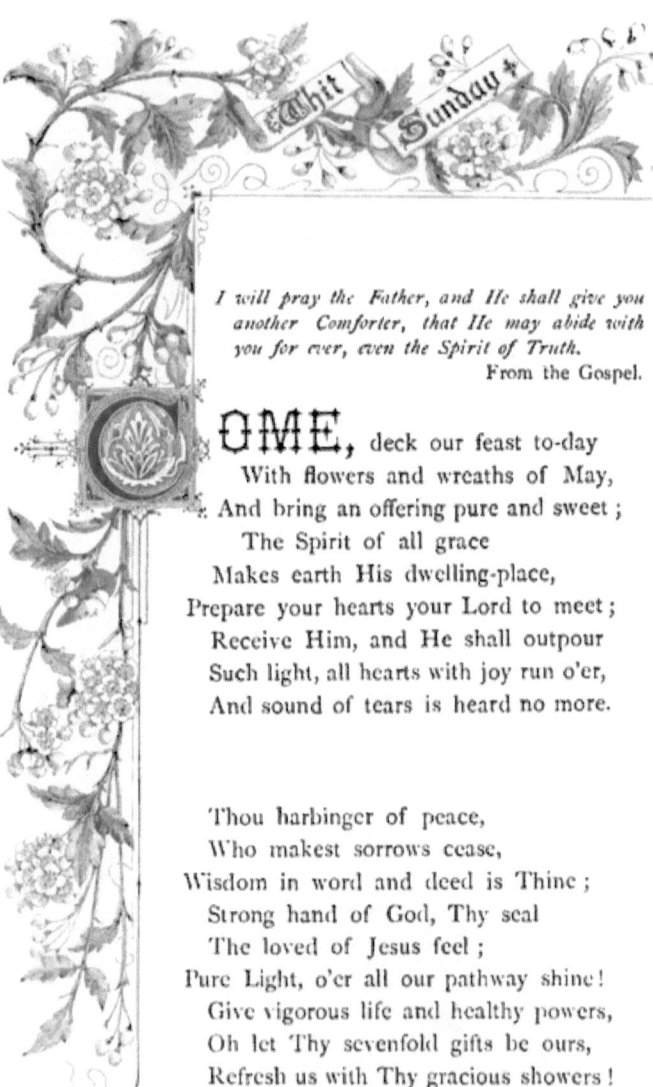

Whit Sunday

I will pray the Father, and He shall give you another Comforter, that He may abide with you for ever, even the Spirit of Truth.

From the Gospel.

COME, deck our feast to-day
   With flowers and wreaths of May,
And bring an offering pure and sweet;
   The Spirit of all grace
   Makes earth His dwelling-place,
Prepare your hearts your Lord to meet;
   Receive Him, and He shall outpour
   Such light, all hearts with joy run o'er,
   And sound of tears is heard no more.

   Thou harbinger of peace,
   Who makest sorrows cease,
Wisdom in word and deed is Thine;
   Strong hand of God, Thy seal
   The loved of Jesus feel;
Pure Light, o'er all our pathway shine!
   Give vigorous life and healthy powers,
   Oh let Thy sevenfold gifts be ours,
   Refresh us with Thy gracious showers!

Oh touch our tongues with flame,
When speaking Jesu's name!
And lead us up the heavenward road.
Give us the power to pray,
Teach us what words to say,
Whene'er we come before our God.
O Highest Good, our spirits cheer,
When raging foes are strong and near,
Give us brave hearts undimm'd by fear.

O golden rain from heaven!
Thy precious dews be given
To bless the churches' barren field!
And let Thy waters flow,
Where'er the sowers sow
The seed of truth, that it may yield
A hundred-fold its living fruit,
O'er all the land may take deep root,
And mighty branches heavenward shoot.

Thou fiery glow of Love!
Let us Thy ardours prove,
Consume our hearts with quenchless fire!
Come, O Thou trackless Wind!
Breathe gently o'er our mind!
Nor let the flesh to rule aspire;
Help us our free-born right to take,
The heavy yoke of sin to break,
And all her tempting paths forsake.

Be it Thine to stir our will;
Our good intents fulfil;
Be with us when we go and come;
Deep in our spirits dwell,
And make their inmost cell
Thy temple pure, Thy holy home!
Teach us to know our Lord, that we
May call His Father ours through Thee,
Thou Pledge of glories yet to be!

Oh make our crosses sweet,
And let Thy sunshine greet
Our longing eyes in clouded hours!
Wing Thou our upward flight
Toward yonder mountain bright,
Girded about with Zion's golden towers!
Forsake us not when our last foe
Puts forth his strength to lay us low,
Then joyful victory bestow!

Let us, while here we dwell,
This one thought ponder well,
That in God's likeness we are made.
As o'er a fruitful land
Rich harvests waving stand,
We, serving Him, bear fruits that never fade,
Till Thou in whom all comfort lies,
Lift us to fields above the skies,
And bid us bloom in Paradise!

SCHMOLCK.

1715.

Monday in Whitsun Week.

Would God that all the Lord's people were prophets,
and that the Lord would put His Spirit upon them!

From the Lesson.

ome to Thy temple here on earth,
　　Be Thou my spirit's guest,
Who givest us of mortal birth
　　A second birth more blest;
Spirit beloved, Thou mighty Lord,
　　Who with the Father and the Son
　　Reignest upon an equal throne,
Art equally adored!

Oh enter, let me feel and know
　　Thy mighty power within,
That can alone our help bestow,
　　And rescue us from sin.
Oh cleanse my soul and make it white,
　　That I with heart unstain'd and true,
　　May daily render service due,
And honour Thee aright.

I was a wild unfruitful vine
　　Which Thou shouldst prune and train;
Death pierced through all this life of mine,
　　But Thou my foe hast slain.
Thy holy baptism is his grave,
　　He perishes beneath the flood
　　Of His most precious death and blood,
Who died our life to save.

Thou art the Spirit who dost teach
  To pray aright, for all
Our prayers are heard if Thou beseech,
  Thy songs have sweetest fall.
They soar on tireless wings to heaven,
  They fail not from before God's throne,
  Till all His goodness we have known
By whom all help is given.

Thou art the Spirit of all joy,
  Sadness Thou lovest not ;
Thy comfort beaming from on high,
  Lights up the darkest lot.
Ah yes, how many a time of old
  Thy voice hath rapt my soul away,
  To yon bright halls of endless day,
And oped the gates of gold !

Thou art the Spirit of all love,
  The Friend of kindly life,
Thou wouldst not that our hearts should prove
  The pangs of wrath and strife.
Thou hatest hatred's withering reign,
  In souls that discord maketh dark
  Dost Thou rekindle love's bright spark,
And make them one again.

On Thee is all this world upstaid,
  And in Thy hands doth rest ;
And Thou canst wayward hearts persuade
  To turn as seems Thee best :

Oh therefore give Thy love and peace,
  That they may join in strongest bands
  Long parted foes, and through our lands
These sad divisions cease.

Thou art the true, the only Source
  Whence concord comes to men;
Oh that Thy power might have free course
  And bring us peace again!
Oh hear, and stem this mighty flood
  That o'er us death and sorrow spreads;
  Alas! each day afresh it sheds
Like water human blood.

And let our nation learn to know
  What, and how deep, our sin;
Nay, let God's judgments come, if so
  A fire be lit within
The hearts that loved themselves to please:
  In bitter shame now let them burn,
  And loving Thee, repentant spurn
Their selfish worldly case.

Grace for the contrite heart abounds,
  Joy to the sad is given;
To serve God's truth will heal our wounds,
  And bring us help from heaven;
Lord, for Thine honour's sake, make known
  Thy power, convert the wicked now,
  And teach the hard to weep, for Thou
Canst soften steel and stone!

Arise and make an end of all
  Our heartache, and our pain ;
Thy wandering flock at last recall
  And grant them joy again ;
To peace and wealth the lands restore,
   Wasted with fire or plague or sword ;
   Come to Thy ruin'd churches, Lord,
And bid them bloom once more !

The rulers of our land defend,
  Our sovereign's throne uphold ;
That he and we may prosper, send
  True wisdom to the old ;
With piety the young men bless,
   And through the nation shed abroad
   True virtue and the fear of God,
A nation's happiness.

Fill every heart with holy zeal
  To keep the faith unstain'd ;
Let house and land Thy blessing feel,
  Whence all true wealth is gain'd.
Him who resists Thy inward powers,
   The Evil Spirit, make Thou flee ;
   Whate'er delights Thy heart, would he
Fain root from out of ours.

Give strong and cheerful hearts to stand
  Undaunted in the wars
That Satan's fierce and mighty band
  Is waging with Thy cause.

Help us to fight as warriors brave,
  That we may conquer in the field,
  And not one Christian man may yield
His soul to sin a slave.

Order according to Thy mind
  Our life from day to day,
And when this life must be resign'd,
  And death has seized his prey,
When all our days have fleeted by,
  Help us to die with fearless spirit,
  And let us after death inherit
Eternal life on high.

PAUL GERHARDT.

DURING THE

YEARS' WAR.

Tuesday in Whitsun-week.

*Hereby know ye the Spirit of God. Every spirit
that confesseth that Jesus Christ is come in
the flesh is of God.*

From the Lesson.

Come Holy Spirit, God and Lord,
    Be all Thy graces now outpour'd
On the believer's mind and soul,
    And touch our hearts with living coal.
Thy Light this day shone forth so clear,
All tongues and nations gather'd near,
To learn that faith, for which we bring
Glad praise to Thee, and loudly sing,

          . Hallelujah, Hallelujah!

Thou Strong Defence, Thou Holy Light,
Teach us to know our God aright,
And call Him Father from the heart:
The Word of life and truth impart,
That we may love not doctrines strange,
Nor e'er to other teachers range,
But Jesus for our Master own
And put our trust in Him alone.

          . Hallelujah, Hallelujah!

Thou Sacred Ardour, Comfort Sweet,
Help us to wait with ready feet
And willing heart at Thy command,
Nor trial fright us from Thy band.
Lord, make us ready with Thy powers,
Strengthen the flesh in weaker hours,
That as good warriors we may force
Through life and death to Thee our course.

          . Hallelujah, Hallelujah!

LUTHER. 1524.

124

Trinity Sunday.

And God said, Let us make man in our image.

From the Lesson.

OST High and Holy Trinity!
    Who of Thy mercy mild
    Hast form'd me here in Time, to be
    Thy image and Thy child:
Oh let me love Thee day and night
With all my soul, with all my might;
Oh come, Thyself my soul prepare,
And make Thy dwelling ever there!

    Father! replenish with Thy grace
    This longing heart of mine,
    Make it Thy quiet dwelling-place,
    Thy sacred inmost shrine!
Forgive that oft my spirit wears
Her time and strength in trivial cares,
Enfold her in Thy changeless peace,
So she from all but Thee may cease!

O God the Son! Thy wisdom's light
   On my dark reason pour;
Forgive that things of sense and sight
   Were all her joy of yore;
Henceforth let every thought and deed
On Thee be fix'd, from Thee proceed,
Draw me to Thee, for I would rise
Above these earthly vanities!

O Holy Ghost! Thou fire of love,
   Enkindle with Thy flame my will;
Come with Thy strength, Lord, from above,
   Help me Thy bidding to fulfil:
Forgive that I so oft have done
What I as sinful ought to shun;
Let me with pure and quenchless fire
Thy favour and Thyself desire!

Most High and Holy Trinity!
   Draw me away far hence,
And fix upon eternity
   All powers of soul and sense!
Make me at one within; at one
With Thee on earth; when life is done
Take me to dwell in light with Thee,
Most High and Holy Trinity!

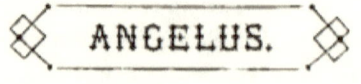

ANGELUS.

1657.

First Sunday after Trinity.

God is Love . . . and herein is love, not that we loved
God, but that He loved us.

From the Epistle.

    wings of faith, ye thoughts, fly hence,
        Roam o'er Eternity's vast field,
    Surpass the bounds of time and sense,
        And rise to Him, who hath reveal'd
    That He is Love : there pause, and awestruck view
    That ancient love with every morning new !

    Ere earth's foundations yet were laid,
        Or heaven's fair roof was spread abroad,
    Ere man a living soul was made,
        Love stirr'd within the heart of God ;
    Love fill'd the long futurity with good,
    And grace to help at need beside her stood.

    'Twas Love whose counsel gave to me
        True life in Christ Thy only Son,
    Whom Thou hast made our Way to Thee,
        From whom all grace flows ever down ;
    Whose sacrifice can make us pure and whole,
    And bless and hallow all our inmost soul.

    'Twas Love, that long ere time began,
        That precious name of child bestow'd ;
    That open'd Heaven on earth to man,
        And call'd us sinners sons of God ;
    Whose gracious promptings move the Father's hand,
    That on the page of life our names may stand :

Ah happy hours, whene'er upsprings
  My soul to yon Eternal Source,
Whence the glad river downward sings,
  Watering with goodness all my course,
So that each passing day anew I prove
How tender and how true my Father's love!

For what am I? At His command
  The million creatures of His power
Start into life on sea and land;
  Oh why should God such blessings shower
On me, who am a leaf that fadeth fast,
A little shifting dust before the blast!

I am not worthy, Lord, that Thou
  Shouldst such compassion on me show;
That He who made the world should bow
  To cheer with love a wretch so low.
O Father, I would utterly resign
Myself to Thee; take me, and make me Thine.

When strength and heart grow faint and sad,
  From battling long with heavy pain,
Thy smile shines forth to make me glad,
  Thou crownest me with joy again;
Then I behold Thy Spirit's wondrous power,
Whose work is mightiest in our weakest hour.

Forth from Thy rich and bounteous store
  Life's common blessings daily flow;
More than we dare to ask, far more

Than we deserve, dost Thou bestow.
My heart dissolves in tears of thankfulness,
To see how true Thy care, how quick to bless.

Nor here alone : hope pierces far
    Through all the shades of earth and time ;
Faith mounts beyond the farthest star,
    Yon shining heights she loves to climb,
And gazing on eternity behold
The promised land, our heritage of old.

Can I with loveless heart receive
    Tokens of love that never cease !
Can I be thankless still, and grieve
    Him who is all my joy and peace !
Ah Friend of Man, were I to turn from Thee,
Myself were sure my own worst enemy.

Could I but honour Thee aright,
    Noble and sweet my song should be,
That earth and heaven should learn Thy might,
    And what my God hath done for me.
There is no music sweet as is Thy name,
No joy so deep as pondering o'er Thy fame.

O heart redeem'd ! thou think'st it long
    Till the appointed hour be come,
When thou shalt join the angels' song
    To that Fair Love that brought thee home.
Have patience, heart : time hurries fast away,
Soon shalt thou reach the one Eternal Day.

                                J. G. HERMANN. 1747.

Second Sunday
after
Trinity.

And this is His commandment; That we should believe on the name of His Son Jesus Christ, and love one another, as He gave us commandment.

From the Epistle.

HEART and heart together bound,
  Seek in God your true repose,
In your love the price be found
  Of your Saviour's love and woes;
We the members, He the Head,
  He the sun, we beams He showers,
Brethren by one Master led,
  We are His, and He is ours.

Children of His realm draw near,
  Make your covenant stronger still,
From your hearts allegiance swear
  Unto Him who conquer'd ill.
If your bonds are yet too weak,
  If but fragile yet they prove,
Help from His good Spirit seek
  Who can steel the chains of love.

Only such love will suffice,
  As the love that dwells in Him,
Love that from the cross ne'er flies,
  Love that spares not life or limb;

'Twas for sinners He was slain,
   'Twas for foes He shed His blood,
That His death for all might gain
   Endless life—the Highest Good.

Thus, O truest Friend, unite
   All Thy consecrated band,
That their hearts be set aright
   To fulfil Thy last command.
Each must onward urge his friend,
   Helping him in word and deed,
Love's blest pathway to ascend,
   Following on where Thou dost lead.

Thou who dost command that all
   Practise love who bear Thy name,
Wake the dead, new followers call,
   Touch the slothful with Thy flame.
Let us live, O Lord, at one,
   As Thou with the Father art,
That through all the world be none
   Of Thy members left apart.

Then were given what Thou hast sought,
   In the Son were all men freed,
And the world at last were taught
   That Thy rule is blest indeed.
Father of all souls, we praise
   Thee who shinest in the Son ;
Lord, to Thee our hymns we raise,
   Who hast all men to Thee drawn !

              After ZINZENDORF.
                    Born 1731.

THIRD SUNDAY
AFTER
TRINITY.

Cast all your care upon Him, for He careth for you.
From the Epistle.

WHAT within me and without,
 Hourly on my spirit weighs,
Burdening heart and soul with doubt,
 Darkening all my weary days:
In it I behold Thy will,
 God, who givest rest and peace,
And my heart is calm and still,
 Waiting till Thou send release.

God! Thou art my rock of strength,
 And my home is in Thine arms,
Thou wilt send me help at length,
 And I feel no wild alarms.
Sin nor Death can pierce the shield
 Thy defence has o'er me thrown,
Up to Thee myself I yield,
 And my sorrows are Thine own.

Thou my shelter from the blast,
 Thou my strong defence art ever;
Though my sorrows thicken fast,
 Yet I know Thou leav'st me never;

When my foe puts forth his might,
    And would tread me in the dust,
To this rock I take my flight,
    And I conquer him through trust.

When my trials tarry long,
  Unto Thee I look and wait,
Knowing none, though keen and strong,
  Can my faith in Thee abate.
And this faith I long have nurst,
  Comes alone, O God, from Thee;
Thou my heart didst open first,
  Thou didst set this hope in me.

Christians! cast on Him your load,
  To your tower of refuge fly;
Know He is the Living God,
  Ever to His creatures nigh.
Seek His ever-open door
  In your hours of utmost need;
All your hearts before Him pour,
  He will send you help with speed.

But hast thou some darling plan,
  Cleaving to the things of earth?
Leanest thou for aid on man?
  Thou wilt find him nothing worth.
Rather trust the One alone
  Whose is endless power and love.
And the help He gives His own,
  Thou in very deed shalt prove.

Yea, on Thee, my God, I rest,
  Letting life float calmly on,
For I know the last is best,
  When the crown of joy is won.

In Thy might all things I bear,
　In Thy love find bitters sweet,
And with all my grief and care
　Sit in patience at Thy feet.

O my soul, why art thou vex'd?
　Let things go as e'en they will;
Though to thee they seem perplex'd,
　Yet His order they fulfil.
Here He is thy strength and guard,
　Power to harm thee here has none;
Yonder will He each reward
　For the works he here has done.

Let Thy mercy's wings be spread
　O'er me, keep me close to Thee,
In the peace Thy love doth shed,
　Let me dwell eternally.
Be my All; in all I do
　Let me only seek Thy will,
Where the heart to Thee is true,
　All is peaceful, calm and still.

A. H. FRANKE.
1663-1727.

Fourth Sunday
After
Trinity.

I reckon that the sufferings of this present time are not worthy to be compared with the glory that shall be revealed in us.

From the Epistle.

WOULDST thou inherit life with Christ
on high?
Then count the cost, and know
That here on earth below
Thou needs must suffer with thy Lord and die.
We reach that gain to which all else is loss,
But through the cross.

Oh think what sorrows Christ Himself has known!
The scorn, and anguish sore,
The bitter death He bore,
Ere He ascended to His heavenly throne;
And deemest thou, thou canst with right complain,
Whate'er thy pain?

Not e'en the sharpest sorrows we can feel,
Nor keenest pangs, we dare
With that great bliss compare
When God His glory shall in us reveal,
That shall endure when our brief woes are o'er
For evermore!

SIMON DACH. 1640.

Fifth Sunday after Trinity.

And who is he that will harm you, if ye be followers of that which is good?
But and if ye suffer for righteousness' sake, happy are ye; and
be not afraid of their terror, neither be troubled;
*but sanctify the **Lord God** in your hearts.*

From the Epistle.

IF GOD be on my side,
    Then let who will oppose,
For oft ere now to Him I cried,
    And he hath quell'd my foes.
    If Jesus be my Friend,
    If God doth love me well,
What matters all my foes intend,
    Though strong they be and fell?

    Here I can firmly rest,
    I dare to boast of this,
That God the Highest and the Best,
    My Friend and Father is.
    From dangerous snares He saves,
    Where'er He bids me go
He checks the storms and calms the waves,
    That nought can work me woe.

    I rest upon the ground
    Of Jesus and His blood,
For 'tis through Him that I have found
    The True Eternal Good.
    Nought have I of mine own,
    Nought in the life I lead,
What Christ hath given me, that alone
    Is worth all love indeed.

His Spirit in me dwells,
O'er all my mind He reigns,
All care and sadness He dispels,
And soothes away all pains.
He prospers day by day
His work within my heart,
Till I have strength and faith to say,
Thou God my Father art!

When weakness on me lies,
And tempts me to despair,
He speaketh words and utters sighs
Of more than mortal prayer;
But what no tongue can tell,
Thou God canst hear and see,
Who readest in the heart full well
If aught there pleaseth Thee.

He whispers in my breast
Sweet words of holy cheer,
How he who seeks in God his rest
Shall ever find Him near;
How God hath built above
A city fair and new,
Where eye and heart shall see and prove
What faith has counted true.

There is prepared on high
My heritage, my lot;
Though here on earth I sink and die,
My heaven shall fail me not.

Though here my days are dark,
And oft my tears must rain,
Whene'er my Saviour's Light I mark,
Lo, all is bright again.

Who joins him to that Lord
Whom Satan flies and hates,
Shall find himself despised, abhorr'd,
For him the burden waits
Of mockery and shame,
Heap'd on his guiltless head;
And crosses, trials, cruel blame,
Shall be his daily bread.

I knew it long ere now,
Yet am I not afraid;
The God to whom I pledged my vow,
Will surely send His aid.
At cost of all I have,
At cost of life and limb,
I cling to God who yet shall save,
I will not turn from Him.

The world may fail and flee,
Thou standest fast for ever,
Nor fire, nor sword, nor plague, from Thee
My trusting soul shall sever.
No hunger, and no thirst,
No poverty or pain,
Let mighty princes do their worst,
Shall fright me back again.

No joys that angels know,
No throne or wide-spread fame,
No love or loss, no fear or woe,
No grief of heart or shame—
Man cannot aught conceive
Of pleasure or of harm,
That e'er could tempt my soul to leave
Her refuge in Thine arm.

My heart for gladness springs,
It cannot more be sad,
For very joy it laughs and sings,
Sees nought but sunshine glad.
The sun that glads mine eyes
Is Christ the Lord I love,
I sing for joy of that which lies
Stored up for us above.

Paul Gerhardt. 1650

Sixth Sunday after Trinity

Know ye not, that so many of us as were baptised into Christ, were baptised into His death?

From the Epistle.

Well for him who all things losing,
  E'en himself doth count as nought,
Still the one thing needful choosing
  That with all true bliss is fraught!

Well for him who nothing knoweth
  But his God, whose boundless love
Makes the heart wherein it gloweth,
  Calm and pure as saints above!

Well for him who all forsaking
  Walketh not in shadows vain,
But the path of peace is taking
  Through this vale of tears and pain!

Oh that we our hearts might sever
  From earth's tempting vanities,
Fixing them on Him for ever
  In whom all our fulness lies!

Oh that we might Him discover
   Whom with longing love we've sought,
Joining us to Him for ever,
   For without Him all is nought!

Oh that ne'er our eyes might wander
   From our God, so might we cease
Ever o'er our sins to ponder,
   And our conscience be at peace!

Thou abyss of love and goodness,
   Draw us by Thy cross to Thee,
That our senses, soul and spirit,
   Ever one with Christ may be!

ANON.

Seventh Sunday
after
Trinity.

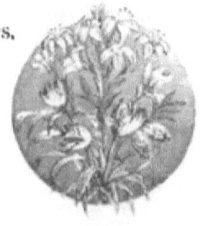

Go forth, my heart, and seek delight
In all the gifts of God's great might,
    These pleasant summer hours :
Look how the plains for thee and me
Have deck'd themselves most fair to see,
    All bright and sweet with flowers.

The trees stand thick and dark with leaves,
And earth o'er all her dust now weaves
    A robe of living green ;
Nor silks of Solomon compare
With glories that the tulips wear,
    Or lilies' spotless sheen.

The lark soars singing into space,
The dove forsakes her hiding-place,
    And coos the woods among ;
The richly-gifted nightingale,
Pours forth her voice o'er hill and dale,
    And floods the fields with song.

Here with her brood the hen doth walk,
There builds and guards his nest the stork,
  The fleet-wing'd swallows pass;
The swift stag leaves his rocky home,
And down the light deer bounding come
  To taste the long rich grass.

The brooks rush gurgling through the sand,
And from the trees on either hand,
  Cool shadows o'er them fall;
The meadows at their side are glad
With herds; and hark! the shepherd lad
  Sends forth his mirthful call.

And humming, hovering to and fro,
The never-wearied swarms now go
  To seek their honey'd food;
And through the vine's yet feeble shoots
Stream daily upwards from her roots
  New strength and juices good.

The corn springs up, a wealth untold,
A sight to gladden young and old,
  Who now their voices lift
To Him who gives such plenteous store,
And makes the cup of life run o'er
  With many a noble gift.

Thy mighty working, mighty God,
Wakes all my powers; I look abroad
  And can no longer rest:
I too must sing when all things sing,
And from my heart the praises ring
  The Highest loveth best.

I think, Art Thou so good to us,
And scatterest joy and beauty thus
  O'er this poor earth of ours;
What nobler glories shall be given
Hereafter in Thy shining heaven,
  Set round with golden towers!

What thrilling joy when on our sight
Christ's garden beams in cloudless light,
  Where all the air is sweet,
Still laden with the unwearied hymn
From all the thousand seraphim
  Who God's high praise repeat!

Oh were I there! Oh that I now,
Dear God, before Thy throne could bow,
  And bear my heavenly palm!
Then like the angels would I raise
My voice, and sing Thy endless praise
  In many a sweet-toned psalm.

Nor can I now, O God, forbear,
Though still this mortal yoke I wear,
  To utter oft Thy name ;
But still my heart is bent to speak
Thy praises ; still, though poor and weak,
  Would I Thy love proclaim.

But help me ; let Thy heavenly showers
Revive and bless my fainting powers,
  And let me thrive and grow
Beneath the summer of Thy grace,
And fruits of faith bud forth apace
  While yet I dwell below.

And set me, Lord, in Paradise
When I have bloom'd beneath these skies
  Till my last leaf is flown ;
Thus let me serve Thee here in time,
And after, in that happier clime,
  And Thee, my God, alone !

Paul Gerhardt.

1659

EIGHTH SUNDAY
AFTER
TRINITY.

*Brethren, we are debtors, not to the flesh, to live
after the flesh. For if ye live after the flesh,
ye shall die; but if ye through the Spirit do
mortify the deeds of the body, ye shall live.*

From the Epistle.

GOD, O Spirit, Light of all that live,
    Who dost on us that sit in darkness shine,
Our darkness ever with Thy Light doth strive,
    In vain Thou lur'st us with Thy beams divine;
Yet none, O Spirit, from Thine eye can hide,
Gladly will I Thy searching glance abide.

Search all my hidden parts, whate'er impure
    Thy Light discovers there, do Thou destroy;
The bitterest pain I willingly endure,
    Such pain is follow'd by eternal joy;
Thou'lt cleanse me from my stains of darkest hue,
And in Christ's image form my soul anew.

I cannot stay the venom'd power of sin,
    'Tis Thy anointing only can avail:
Oh make my spirit new and right within,
    Without Thee all my utmost efforts fail.
Life to my cold dead soul I cannot give,
Be Thou my life, so only shall I live.

O Breath from out the Eternal Silence, blow
  All softly o'er my spirit's barren ground,
The precious fulness of my God bestow,
  That where erst sin and shame alone were found,
Faith, love, and holy reverence may upspring,
In spirit and in truth to worship God our King.

Oh let my thoughts, my actions and my will
  Obedient solely to Thy impulse move,
My heart and senses keep Thou blameless still,
  Fix'd and absorb'd in God's unutter'd love.
Thy praying, teaching, striving, in my heart,
Let me not quench, nor make Thee to depart.

O Fount, O Spirit, who dost take and show
  Things of the Son to us, who crystal clear
From God's throne and the Lamb's doth ceaseless flow
  Into the quiet hearts that seek Thee here,
I open wide my mouth, and thirsting sink
Beside Thy stream, its living waves to drink.

I give myself to Thee, to Thee alone,
  From all else sunder'd, Thou art ever near,
The creature and myself I all disown,
  Trusting with inmost faith that God is here!
O God, O Spirit, Light of Life, we see
None ever wait in vain, who wait for Thee.

TERSTEEGEN.

1731.

Ninth Sunday after Trinity.

How long halt ye between two opinions? If the Lord be God, follow Him; but if Baal, then follow him.

From the Lesson.

HY halt thus, O deluded heart,
Why waver longer in
thy choice?
Is it so hard to choose
the part
Offer'd by Heaven's
entreating voice?
Oh look with clearer
eyes again,
Nor strive to enter in,
in vain.
Press on!

Remember, 'tis not
Cæsar's throne,
Nor earthly honour,
wealth or might,
Whereby God's favour
shall be shown
To him who conquers
in this fight:
Himself and an eternity
Of bliss and rest He
offers thee.
Press on!

God crowneth no divided heart;
   To Him oh hallow all thy life!
Who loveth Jesus but in part,
   He works himself much pain and strife,
And gains what he deserveth well,
Here conflict, and hereafter hell.
                 Press on!

Who wrestling long, with many a cry
   Can bid farewell at last to all,
Yet ever loves the Lord most High,
   Loves Him alone whate'er befall,
Is counted worthy of the crown,
And on a kingly throne set down.
                 Press on!

Then break the rotten bonds away
   That hinder you your race to run,
That make you linger oft and stay;
   Oh be your course afresh begun!
Let no false rest your soul deceive,
Up! 'tis a Heaven ye must achieve!
                 Press on!

Omnipotence is on your side,
   And Wisdom watches o'er your heads,
And God Himself will be your guide
   So ye but follow where He leads;
How many guided by His hand,
Have reach'd ere now their father-land!
                 Press on!

Nor let the body dull the soul,
　Its weakness, fears, and sloth despise;
Man toils and roams from pole to pole
　To gain some earthly fleeting prize,
The Highest Good he little cares
To win, or striving soon despairs.
　　　　　　　　Press on!

Oh help each other, hasten on,
　Behold the goal is nigh at hand;
The battle-field shall soon be won,
　Your King shall soon before you stand!
To calmest rest He leads you now,
And sets His crown upon your brow.
　　　　　　　　Press on!

Tenth Sunday After Trinity

As the hart panteth after the water brooks, even so panteth my soul after Thee, O God.

Psalm xlii. 1.

O GOD, I long Thy Light to see,
My God, I hourly think on Thee;
Oh draw me up, nor hide Thy face,
But help me from Thy holy place.

As toward her sun the sunflower turns,
Towards Thee, my Sun, my spirit yearns;
Oh would that free from sin I might
Thus follow evermore Thy Light!

But sin hath so within me wrought,
Such deadly sickness on me brought,
My languid soul sits drooping here
And cannot reach the heavenly sphere.

LYRA GERMANICA.

Ah how shall I my freedom win ?
How break this heavy yoke of sin ?
My fainting spirit thirsts for 'Thee,
Come, Lord, to help and set me free.

My heart is set to do Thy will,
But all my deeds are faulty still ;
My best attempts are nothing worth,
But soil'd with cleaving taint of earth.

Remember that I am Thy child,
Forgive whate'er my soul defiled,
Blot out my sins, that I may rise
Freely to Thee beyond the skies.

Help me to love the world no more,
Be Master of my house and store,
The shield of faith around me throw,
And break the arrows of my foe.

Fain would my heart henceforward be
Fix'd, O my God, alone on Thee,
That heart and soul by Thee possest,
May find in Thee their perfect rest.

Begone, ye pleasures false and vain,
Untasted, undesired remain !
In heaven alone those joys abound,
Where all my true delight is found.

Oh take away whate'er has stood
Between me and the Highest Good ;
I ask no better boon than this,
To find in God my only bliss.

ANTON ULRICH,
Duke of Brunswick. 1667.

Eleventh Sunday
after
Trinity.

*In Thy presence is fulness of joy; at Thy right hand
there are pleasures for evermore.*

Psalm xvi. 12.

FRIEND of souls, how well is me,
  Whene'er Thy love my spirit calms!
From sorrow's dungeon forth I flee,
  And hide me in Thy shelt'ring arms.
The night of weeping flies away
Before the heart-reviving ray
  Of love, that beams from out Thy breast;
Here is my heaven on earth begun;
Who were not joyful had he won
  In Thee, O God, his joy and rest!

The world may call herself my foe,
  So be it; for I trust her not,
E'en though a friendly face she show,
  And with her bounties heap my lot.
In Thee alone will I rejoice,
Thou art the Friend, Lord, of my choice,
  For Thou art true when friendships fail;
'Mid storms of woe Thy truth is still
My anchor; hate me as it will,
  The world shall o'er me ne'er prevail.

LYRA GERMANICA.

Through deserts of the cross Thou leadest,
  I follow leaning on Thy hand;
From out the clouds Thy child Thou feedest,
  And giv'st him water from the sand.
I know Thy wondrous ways will end
In love and blessing, Thou true Friend,
  Enough if Thou art ever near!
I know, whom Thou wilt glorify,
And raise o'er sun and stars on high,
  Thou lead'st through depths and darkness here.

To others Death seems dark and grim,
  But not, Thou Life of life, to me;
I know Thou ne'er forsakest him
  Whose heart and spirit rest in Thee.
Oh who would fear his journey's close,
If from dark woods and lurking foes,
  He then found safety and release!
Nay, rather with a joyful heart
From this dark region I depart
  To Thy eternal light and peace.

O Friend of souls, then well indeed
  Is me, when on Thy love I lean!
The world, nor pain, nor death I heed,
  Since Thou, my God, my joy hast been.
Oh let this peace that Thou hast given
Be but a foretaste of Thy heaven,
  For goodness infinite is Thine.
Hence, world, with all thy flattering toys!
In God alone lie all my joys;
  Oh rich delight, my Friend is mine!

Deszler. 1692.

TWELFTH SUNDAY AFTER TRINITY.

Not that we are sufficient of ourselves to think anything as of ourselves, but our sufficiency is of God.

From the Epistle.

WHO seeks in weakness an excuse,
His sins will vanquish never;
Unless he heart and mind renews,
He is deceived for ever.
The strait and narrow way,
That shines to perfect day,
He hath not found, hath never trod;
Little he knows, I ween,
What prayer and conflict mean
To one who hath the light of God.

In what the world calls weakness lurks
The very strength of evil,
Full mightily it helps the works
Of our great foe the devil.
Awake, my soul, awake,
Thy refuge quickly take
With Him, the Almighty, who can save;
One look from Christ thy Lord
Can sever every cord
That binds thee now, a wretched slave.

Know, the first step in Christian lore
  Is to depart from sin ;
True faith will leave the world no more
  A place thy heart within.
    Thy Saviour's Spirit first
    The heavy bonds must burst,
  Wherein Death bound thee in thy need ;
    Then the freed spirit knows
    What strength He gives to those
  Who with their Lord are risen indeed.

And what Thy Spirit, Lord, began
  Help Thou with inner might !
Earth has no better gift for man
  Than strength and love of right.
    Oh make Thy followers just
    Who look to Thee in trust,
  Thy strength and justice let us know :
    Our souls through Thee would wear
    The power of grace, most fair
  Of all the jewels faith can show.

Strong Son of God, break down Thy foes,
  So shall we conquer ours ;
Strong in the might from Thee that flows.
  We mourn not lack of powers,
    E'er since that from above,
    The witness of Thy love
  Thy Spirit came, and doth abide
    With us, dispelling fear
    And falsehood, that we here
  May fight and conquer on Thy side.

Give strength, whene'er our strength must fail;
　Give strength the flesh to curb;
Give strength when craft and sin prevail
　To weaken and disturb.
　　The world doth lay her snares
　　To catch us unawares,
　Give strength to sweep them all away;
　　So in our utmost need,
　　And when death comes indeed,
　Thy strength shall be our perfect stay.

THIRTEENTH SUNDAY
AFTER TRINITY.

Then Hezekiah received the letter of the hands of the messengers, and read it, and Hezekiah went up into the house of the Lord, and spread it before the Lord.

From the Lesson.

LEAVE God to order all thy ways,
　　And hope in Him whate'er betide,
Thou'lt find Him in the evil days
　　Thy all-sufficient strength and guide ;
Who trusts in God's unchanging love,
Builds on the rock that nought can move.

What can these anxious cares avail,
　　These never-ceasing moans and sighs ?
What can it help us to bewail
　　Each painful moment as it flies ?
Our cross and trials do but press
The heavier for our bitterness.

Only thy restless heart keep still,
　　And wait in cheerful hope ; content
To take whate'er His gracious will,
　　His all-discerning love hath sent ;
Nor doubt our inmost wants are known
To Him who chose us for His own.

He knows when joyful hours are best.
　　He sends them as He sees it meet :
When thou hast borne the fiery test,

And now art freed from all deceit,
He comes to thee all unaware,
And makes thee own His loving care.

Nor in the heat of pain and strife,
  Think God hath cast thee off unheard,
And that the man, whose prosperous life
  Thou enviest, is of Him preferr'd;
Time passes and much change doth bring.
And sets a bound to everything.

All are alike before His face;
  'Tis easy to our God most High
To make the rich man poor and base,
  To give the poor man wealth and joy.
True wonders still by Him are wrought,
Who setteth up, and brings to nought.

Sing, pray, and swerve not from His ways,
  But do thine own part faithfully,
Trust His rich promises of grace,
  So shall they be fulfill'd in thee;
God never yet forsook at need
The soul that trusted Him indeed.

FOURTEENTH SUNDAY
AFTER TRINITY.

*And they that are Christ's have crucified the flesh
with the affections and lusts.*

From the Epistle.

CROSS, we hail thy bitter reign,
O come, thou well-beloved guest!
Whose sorest sufferings work not pain,
Whose heaviest burden is but rest.

For is not our Redeemer bound
In closest ties of love to those
Who faithful to the cross are found,
Through ceaseless tears, through saddest woes?

Hark, the confessors of the faith
Yet of their cross and fetters boast;
All saints have borne it to the death,
With all the martyrs' radiant host.

Pledge of our glorious home afar!
Thee, Holy Sign, with joy we take,
Sign of a peace life could not mar,
Of just content death could not shake:

The Sign how Truth, once crucified,
   Now throned in majesty doth reign,
How Love is bless'd and glorified,
   That here on earth was mock'd and slain.

Their names are writ in words of light
   Who here on earth their Lord confest;
They hear the bridegroom's cry at night,
   Come to my marriage feast, ye blest!

Who then would faint, nor join to share
   In Christ's reproach, in want or pain?
The bitterest death who would not dare?
   Who fears a martyr's crown to gain?

Up, Brethren of the Cross! and haste
   Where Christ our Head hath gone before!
We hymn His praise the while we taste
   The shame and death He sometime bore.

In bonds and stripes, in falsest blame,
   Our crown, our dearest wealth we see,
A dungeon were a throne, and shame
   Our chiefest glory, borne for Thee.

What though the world on us may fling
   Its scorn, and oft we strive with death,
The holy angels speed to bring
   Our help and strength, our victor's wreath.

Up, quit the gates where sin abides,
   From earth's doom'd cities quickly come,
Yon eastern Star full surely guides
   All pilgrims to their Father's home.

               GOTTER.

                 1697.

FIFTEENTH SUNDAY
AFTER TRINITY.

Therefore take no thought, saying, What shall we eat, or what shall we drink
.. for your Heavenly Father knoweth that ye have need of all these things.

From the Gospel.

BE thou content; be still before
    His face, at whose right hand doth reign
Fulness of joy for evermore,
    Without whom all thy toil is vain.
He is thy living spring, thy sun, whose rays
Make glad with life and light thy dreary days.
Be thou content.

In Him is comfort, light and grace,
    And changeless love beyond our thought;
The sorest pang, the worst disgrace,
    If He is there, shall harm thee not.
He can lift off thy cross, and loose thy bands,
And calm thy fears, nay, death is in His hands.
Be thou content.

Or art thou friendless and alone,
    Hast none in whom thou canst confide?
God careth for thee, lonely one,
    Comfort and help will He provide.
He sees thy sorrows and thy hidden grief,
He knoweth when to send thee quick relief;
Be thou content.

Thy heart's unspoken pain He knows,
    Thy secret sighs He hears full well,
What to none else thou dar'st disclose,
    To Him thou mayst with boldness tell:

He is not far away, but ever nigh,
And answereth willingly the poor man's cry.
> Be thou content.

Be not o'er-master'd by thy pain,
   But cling to God, thou shalt not fall;
The floods sweep over thee in vain,
   Thou yet shalt rise above them all;
For when thy trial seems too hard to bear,
Lo! God, thy King, hath granted all thy prayer:
> Be thou content.

Why art thou full of anxious fear
   How thou shalt be sustain'd and fed?
He who hath made and placed thee here,
   Will give thee needful daily bread;
Canst thou not trust His rich and bounteous hand,
Who feeds all living things on sea and land?
> Be thou content.

He who doth teach the little birds
   To find their meat in field and wood,
Who gives the countless flocks and herds
   Each day their needful drink and food,
Thy hunger too will surely satisfy,
And all thy wants in His good time supply.
> Be thou content.

Sayst thou, I know not how or where,
   No help I see where'er I turn;
When of all else we most despair,
   The riches of God's love we learn;
When thou and I His hand no longer trace,
He leads us forth into a pleasant place.
> Be thou content.

Though long His promised aid delay,
   At last it will be surely sent:
Though thy heart sink in sore dismay,
   The trial for thy good is meant.
What we have won with pains we hold more fast,
What tarrieth long is sweeter at the last.
                Be thou content.

Lay not to heart whate'er of ill
   Thy foes may falsely speak of thee,
Let man defame thee as he will,
   God hears, and judges righteously.
Why shouldst thou fear, if God be on thy side,
Man's cruel anger, or malicious pride?
                Be thou content.

We know for us a rest remains,
   When God will give us sweet release
From earth and all our mortal chains,
   And turn our sufferings into peace.
Sooner or later death will surely come
To end our sorrows, and to take us home:
                Be thou content.

Home to the chosen ones, who here
   Served their Lord faithfully and well,
Who died in peace, without a fear,
   And there in peace for ever dwell;
The Everlasting is their joy and stay,
The Eternal Word Himself to them doth say,
                Be thou content!

PAUL GERHARDT.

1670.

SIXTEENTH SUNDAY
AFTER TRINITY.

And when the Lord saw her, He had compassion on her, and said unto her, Weep not!

From the Gospel.

LEAVE all to God,
   Forsaken one, and stay thy tears;
For the Highest knows thy pain,
   Sees thy sufferings and thy fears
Thou shalt not wait His help in vain,
   Leave all to God.

Be still and trust !
For His strokes are strokes of love,
  Thou must for thy profit bear;
He thy filial fear would move,
  Trust thy Father's loving care,
    Be still and trust !

  Know, God is near !
Though thou think Him far away,
  Though His mercy long have slept,
He will come and not delay,
  When His child enough hath wept,
    For God is near !

  Oh teach Him not
When and how to hear thy prayers;
  Never doth our God forget,
He the cross who longest bears
  Finds his sorrows' bounds are set,
    Then teach Him not.

  If thou love Him,
Walking truly in His ways,
  Then no trouble, cross or death,
E'er shall silence faith and praise;
  All things serve thee here beneath,
    If thou love God !

            ANTON ULRICH,
              Duke of Brunswick.

                  1667.

Seventeenth Sunday After Trinity

I beseech you that ye walk worthy of the vocation wherewith ye are called, with all lowliness and meekness, with long suffering, forbearing one another in love; endeavouring to keep the unity of the spirit in the bond of peace.

From the Epistle.

COME brethren, let us go!
The evening closeth round,
'Tis perilous to linger here
On this wild desert ground.
Come, towards eternity
Press on from strength to strength,
Nor dread your journey's toils nor length,
For good its end shall be.

We shall not rue our choice,
Though straight our path and steep,
We know that He who call'd us here
His word shall ever keep.

Then follow, trusting; come,
And let each set his face
Toward yonder fair and blessed place,
Intent to reach our home.

The body and the house
Deck not, but deck the heart
With all your powers; we are but guests,
Ere long we must depart.
Ease brings disease; content
Howe'er his lot may fall,
A pilgrim bears and bows to all,
For soon the time is spent.

Come, children, let us go!
Our Father is our guide;
And when the way grows steep and dark,
He journeys at our side.
Our spirits He would cheer,
The sunshine of His love
Revives and helps us as we rove,
Ah, blest our lot e'en here!

Each hasten bravely on,
Not yet our goal is near:
Look to the fiery pillar oft,
That tells the Lord is here.
Your glances onward send,
Love beckons us, nor think
That they who following chance to sink
Shall miss their journey's end.

Come, children, let us go!
We travel hand in hand;
Each in his brother finds his joy
In this wild stranger land.
As children let us be,
Nor by the way fall out,
The angels guard us round about,
And help us brotherly.

The strong be quick to raise
The weaker when they fall;
Let love and peace and patience bloom
In ready help for all.
In love yet closer bound,
Each would be least, yet still
On love's fair path most pure from ill,
Most loving, would be found.

Come, wander on with joy,
For shorter grows the way,
The hour that frees us from the flesh
Draws nearer day by day.
A little truth and love,
A little courage yet,
More free from earth, more apt to set
Your hopes on things above.

It will not last for long,
A little farther roam;
It will not last much longer now
Ere we shall reach our home;

There shall we ever rest,
There with our Father dwell,
With all the saints who served Him well,
There truly, deeply blest.

For this all things we dare,—
'Tis worth the risk I trow,—
Renouncing all that clogs our course,
Or weighs us down below.
O world, thou art too small,
We seek another higher,
Whither Christ guides us ever nigher,
Where God is all in all.

Friend of our perfect choice,
Thou Joy of all that live,
Being that know'st not chance or change,
What courage dost Thou give!
All beauty, Lord, we see,
All bliss and life and love,
In Him in whom we live and move,
And we are glad in Thee!

TERSTEEGEN.
1731.

Eighteenth Sunday after Trinity.

Waiting for the coming of our Lord Jesus Christ, who shall also confirm you unto the end.

From the Epistle.

THOUGH
all to Thee
were faithless,
I yet were true, my Head,
To show that love is deathless,
  From earth not wholly
    fled.

Here didst Thou live in sadness,
  And die in pain for me,
For this I give with gladness
  My heart and soul to Thee.

I could weep night and morning
  That Thou hast died, and yet
So few will heed Thy warning,
  So many Thee forget.

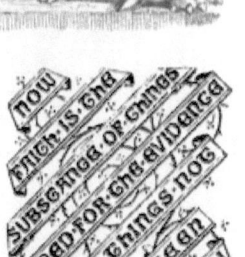

O loving and true-hearted,
  How much for us didst Thou!
Yet is Thy fame departed,
  And none regards it now.

But still Thy love befriends us,
  Of every heart the guide;
Unfailing help it lends us,
  Though all had turn'd aside.
Oh! such love soon or later
  Must conquer, must be felt,
Then at Thy feet the traitor
  In bitter tears shall melt.

Lord, I have inly found Thee,
  Depart Thou not from me,
But wrap Thy love around me,
  And keep me close to Thee.
Once too my brethren, yonder
  Upgazing where Thou art,
Shall learn Thy love with wonder,
  And sink upon Thy heart.

.∴.

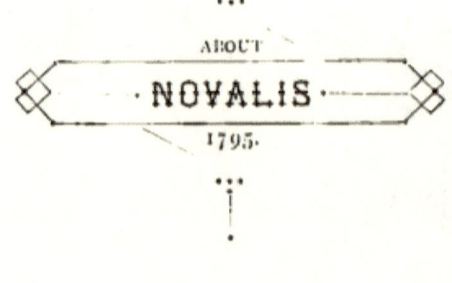

ABOUT

· NOVALIS ·

1795.

NINETEENTH SUNDAY
AFTER TRINITY.

*But ye have not so learned Christ; if so be that ye
have heard Him, and have been taught by Him,
as the truth is in Jesus: that ye put off, concerning the former conversation, the old man,
which is corrupt according to the deceitful lusts;
and be renewed in the spirit of your mind; and
that ye put on the new man, which after God
is created in righteousness and true holiness.*

From the Epistle.

Oh well for him who all things braves,
 A soldier of the Lord to be,
Whom vice counts not among her slaves,
 From envy, pride, and passion free;
Who wars against the world of sin
Without him, and self-will within.

Who follows Christ whate'er betide,
 Is worthy of a soldier's name;
Is He thy Way, thy Light, thy Guide,
 'Tis meet thou also bear His shame:
Who shrinks from dark Gethsemane,
Shall Tabor's glories never see.

What profits it that Christ hath deign'd
 To wear our mortal nature thus,
If we ourselves have ne'er attain'd
 That God reveal Himself in us?
The pure and virgin soul alone
He chooseth for His earthly throne.

175

What profits it that Christ is born,
  And bringeth childhood back to men,
Unless our long-lost right we mourn,
  And win through penitence again,
And lead a God-like life on earth,
As children of the second birth?

What profits all that Christ hath taught,
  If man is slave to reason still,
And worldly wisdom, honour, thought,
  Rule all his acts, and move his will?
He follows what his Lord doth teach
Who true denial of self would reach.

What profit us His deeds and life,
  His meekness, love so quick to bless,
If we give place to pride and strife,
  Dishonouring thus His holiness?
What profits it, if for reward,
And not in faith, we call Him Lord?

What profits us His agony,
  If we endure not pain and scorn?
'Tis combat brings forth victory,
  Of sorrow sweetest joys are born;
And ne'er to him Christ's crown is given,
Who hath not here with Adam striven.

What profit ye His death and cross,
  Unless to self ye also die?
Ye love your life to find it loss,

Afraid the flesh to crucify.
Wouldst live to this world still ? Then know,
His death to thee is barren show.

What profit that He loosed and broke
  All bonds, if ye in league remain
With earth ? Who weareth Satan's yoke
  Shall call Him Master but in vain.
Count ye the soul for reconciled,
Yet slave to earth, by sin defiled ?

What profits it that He is risen,
  If dead in sins thou yet dost lie !
If yet thou cleavest to thy prison,
  What profit that He dwells on high ?
His triumph will avail thee nought,
If thou hast ne'er the battle fought.

Then live and suffer, do and bear,
  As Christ thy pattern here hath done,
And seek His innocence to wear,
  That He may count thee of His own.
Who loveth Christ cares but to win
New triumphs o'er the world of sin.

ANON.

TWENTIETH SUNDAY AFTER TRINITY.

Singing and making melody in your heart unto the Lord; giving thanks always for all things unto God and the Father, in the name of our Lord Jesus Christ.

From the Epistle.

Oh would I had a thousand tongues,
    To sound Thy praise o'er land and sea!
Oh! rich and sweet should be my songs,
    Of all my God has done for me!
With thankfulness my heart must often swell,
But mortal lips Thy praises faintly tell.

Oh that my voice could far resound
    Up to yon stars that o'er me shine!
Would that my blood for joy might bound
    Through every vein while life is mine!
Would that each pulse were gratitude, each breath
A song to Him who keeps me safe from death!

O all ye powers of soul and mind,
    Arise, keep silence thus no more;
Put forth your strength, and ye shall find
    Your noblest work is to adore.
O soul and body, make ye pure and meet,
With heartfelt praise your God and Lord to greet.

Ye little leaves so fresh and green,
    That dance for joy in summer air,
Ye slender grasses, bright and keen,
    Ye flowers so wondrous sweet and fair ;
Ye only for your Maker's glory live,
Help me, for all His love, meet praise to give.

O all ye living things that throng
    With breath and motion earth and sky,
Be ye companions in my song,
    Help me to raise His praises high ;
For my unaided powers are far too weak
The glories of His mighty works to speak.

And first, O Father, praise to Thee
    For all I am and all I have,
It was Thy merciful decree

That all those blessings richly gave,
Which o'er the earth are scatter'd far and near,
To help and gladden us who sojourn here.

And, dearest Jesus, blest be Thou,
    Whose heart with pity overflows,
  Thou rich in help! who deign'dst to bow
    To earth, and taste her keenest woes;
Thy death has burst my bonds and set me free,
Has made me Thine; henceforth I cling to Thee.

  Nor less to Thee, O Holy Ghost,
    Be everlasting honours paid,
  For all Thy comfort, Lord, and most
    That I a child of life am made
By Thy deep lore; my good deeds are not mine,
Thou workest them through me, O Light Divine.

  Yes, Lord, through all my changing days,
    With each new scene afresh I mark
  How wondrously Thou guid'st my ways,
    Where all seems troubled, wilder'd, dark:
When dangers thicken fast, and hopes depart,
Thy light beams comfort on my sinking heart.

  Shall I not then be fill'd with joy,
    Shall I not praise Thee evermore?
  Triumphant songs my lips employ,
    E'en when my cup of woe runs o'er;
Nay, though the heavens should vanish as a scroll,
Nothing shall shake or daunt my trusting soul.

But of Thy goodness will I sing
 As long as I have life and breath,
Offerings of thanks I'll daily bring
 Until my heart is still in death;
And when at last my lips grow pale and cold,
Yet in my sighs Thy praises shall be told.

Father, do Thou in mercy deign
 To listen to my earthly lays;
Once shall I learn a nobler strain,
 Where angels ever hymn Thy praise,
There in the radiant choir I too shall sing
Loud hallelujahs to my glorious King.

Twenty-first Sunday after Trinity.

A SURE stronghold our God is He,
A trusty shield and weapon;
Our help He'll be and set us free
From every ill can happen.
That old malicious foe
Intends us deadly woe : | And deepest craft as well,
Arm'd with the strength of hell | On earth is not his fellow.

BE
STRONG
IN THE LORD,
AND IN THE
POWER OF
HIS MIGHT.
PUT ON
THE WHOLE
ARMOUR OF
GOD,
THAT YE
MAY BE ABLE
TO STAND
AGAINST THE
WILES OF
THE DEVIL.
FOR
WE WRESTLE
NOT AGAINST
FLESH AND
BLOOD,
BUT AGAINST
PRINCIPALITIES,
AGAINST POWERS,
AGAINST
THE RULERS
OF THE
DARKNESS
OF
THIS WORLD,
AGAINST
SPIRITUAL
WICKEDNESS
IN
HIGH PLACES.

*From the
Epistle.*

Through our own force we nothing can,
  Straight were we lost for ever;
But for us fights the proper Man,
  By God sent to deliver.
Ask ye who this may be?
Christ Jesus named is He,
Of Sabaoth the Lord;
Sole God to be adored;
'Tis he must win the battle.

And were the world with devils fill'd,
  All eager to devour us,
Our souls to fear should little yield,
  They cannot overpower us.
Their dreaded Prince no more
Can harm us as of yore;
Look grim as e'er he may,
Doom'd is his ancient sway;
A word can overthrow him.

Still shall they leave that Word His might.
  And yet no thanks shall merit;
Still is He with us in the fight,
  By His good gifts and Spirit.
E'en should they take our life,
Goods, honour, children, wife—
Though all of these be gone,
Yet nothing have they won,
God's kingdom ours abideth!

LUTHER.

Hymn composed on the road to Worms.
1530.

Twenty-second Sunday After Trinity.

Trust in the Lord with all thine heart, and lean not unto thine own understanding.

From the Lesson.

OW blest to all Thy followers, Lord, the road
    By which Thou lead'st them on, yet oft how strange!
But Thou in all dost seek our highest good,
    For Truth were true no longer, couldst Thou change.
Though crooked seem the paths, yet are they straight,
    By which Thou draw'st Thy children up to Thee,
    And passing wonders by the way they see,
And learn at last to own Thee wise and great.

No human laws can bind Thy Spirit, Lord,
    That reason or opinion frame for us;
The knot of doubt is sever'd by Thy sword,
    Or falls unravell'd if Thou willest thus.
The strongest bonds are weak to Thee, O God,
    All sinks and fails that would Thy course oppose:
    Thy lightest word can quell Thy stoutest foes,
And desert paths are by Thy footsteps trod.

What human prudence fondly strives to bind,
    Thy wisdom sunders far as east from west:
Who long beneath the yoke of man have pined,
    Thy hand exalteth high above the rest.

The world would scatter, Thou dost union give;
  She breaks, Thou buildest; what she builds is made
  A ruin'd heap; her light is nought but shade;
Her dead Thy Spirit calls to rise and live.

Is there an act our reason would applaud?
  Lo! in Thy book hast Thou the example given;
But him whom none as wise and pious laud,
  Thou often lead'st in secret up to Heaven,
As Thou didst leave the Pharisee, to go
  And eat with sinners whom all else forsook.
  Who can search out Thy purposes, or look
Into the abyss of wisdom whence they flow?

Our all, O God, is nothing in Thine eyes,
  Our nothing Thou regardest oft with love;
Glory and pomp of words Thou dost not prize,
  Thy impulse only gives them power to move.
Thy noblest works awaken not man's praise,
  For they are hidden, and he blindly turns
  Away, nor though he see, their light discerns,
Too gross his sense, too keen their dazzling rays.

O Ruler! We would bless Thee and adore,
  At whose command we live or turn to dust;
When Thou dost give us of Thy wisdom's store,
  We see how true Thy care, and learn to trust.
Thy wisdom plays with us as with a child,
  Who playing learns his Father loves him well;
  'Tis love that brings Thee down with man to dwell,
Love guides our faltering footsteps through the wild.

Now seems to us o'er harsh and strict Thy school,
  Now dost Thou greet us mild and tenderly,
Now when our wilder passions break Thy rule,
  Thy judgments fright us back again to Thee.
With downcast eyes we seek Thy face again,
  Thou kissest us, we promise fair amends,
  Once more Thy Spirit rest and pardon sends,
And curbs our passions with a stronger rein.

Thou know'st, O Father, all our weakness well,
  Our impotence, our foolishness of mind;
Almost a passing glance may serve to tell
  How weak are we, how ignorant, how blind,
And so Thou comest with Thy help and stay,
  A father's rule, a mother's love are Thine;
  The lamb, on whom none else discern Thy sign,
Thou carriest in Thy bosom day by day.

The common ways are trodden not of Thee,
  Thy steps are seldom traced by mortal eyes,
Yet art Thou near us, and unseen, dost see
  All hopes and wishes that within us rise.
The bright reflection of Thy inner thought
  Is day by day before our eyes outspread;
  Who thinks he quickest hath Thy meaning read,
Is oft another deeper lesson taught.

O Eye, whose glance no falsehood can endure,
  Grant me to wisely judge, and well discern
Nature from grace—Thy Light serene and pure
  From grosser fires that in and round me burn.
Let no strange fire be kindled on the shrine
  Within my heart, lest I should madly bring
  The hated offering unto Thee, O King.
Ah, blest the soul whose light is born of Thine!

When reason contradicts Thy law, or climbs
  So high, she weeneth to know more than Thou,
Break down her confidence, great God, betimes,
  And teach her lowly at Thy feet to bow.
Nor let my proud heart dictate, Lord, to Thee,
  But tame the wayward will that seeks its own,
  And wake the love that clings to Thee alone,
And takes Thy judgments in humility.

Absorb my will in Thine; support and bear
  Onward in loving arms Thy timid child;
Thy Spirit's voice dispels all doubt, all fear,
  And quells the passions erst so fierce and wild.
Thou art mine All, since that Thy Son is mine;
  Oh let Thy Spirit work with power in me,
  With strong desire I thirst, I pant for Thee,
Oh joy whene'er Thy glories round me shine!

So shall the creature ever serve me here,
  Nor angels blush to bear me company;
The perfect spirits to Thy throne most near,
  They are my brethren, waiting there for me;
And oft my spirit joys to meet a heart,
  That loveth Thee and me and every saint.
  Is aught then left can make me sad and faint?
Come, Fount of Joy! vain sorrows, all depart!

GOTTFRIED ARNOLD. 1666-1714.

Twenty-third Sunday after Trinity.

For our conversation is in heaven; from whence also
we look for the Saviour, the Lord Jesus Christ;
who shall change our vile body, that it may be
fashioned like unto His glorious body, according to
the working whereby He is able even to subdue all
things unto Himself.

From the Epistle.

HE who will in thee rejoice,
   O thou fair and wondrous earth!
Ever anguish'd sorrow's voice
   Pierces through thy seeming mirth;
Let thy vain delights be given
Unto them who love not Heaven,
My desire is fix'd on Thee,
Jesus, dearest far to me!

Weary souls with toil outworn,
   Drooping 'neath the glaring light,
Wish that soon the coming morn
   Might be quench'd again in night,
That their toils might find a close
In a soft and deep repose:
I but wish to rest in Thee,
Jesus, dearest far to me!

Others dare the treacherous wave,
  Hidden rock and shifting wind—
Storm and danger let them brave,
  Earthly good or wealth to find ;
Faith shall wing my upward flight
Far above yon starry height,
Till I find myself with Thee,
Jesus, dearest Friend to me !

Many a time ere now I said,
  Many a time again shall say,
Would to God that I were dead,
  Would that in my grave I lay !
Rest were mine, and sweet my lot
Where the body hindereth not,
And the soul can ever be,
Jesus, dearest Lord, with Thee !

Come, O Death, thou twin of Sleep,
  Lead me hence,—I pray thee come,
Loose my rudder, through the deep
  Guide my vessel safely home.
Thy approach who will may fly,
'Twere a joy to me to die,
Death but opes the gates to Thee,
Jesus, dearest Friend to me !

Would that I to-day might leave
  This my earthly prison here,
And my crown of joy receive
  Waiting me in yon bright sphere !

In that home of joy, where dwell
Hosts of angels, would I tell
How the Godhead shines in Thee,
Jesus, dearest Lord to me!

But not yet the gates of gold
   I may see nor enter in,
Nor the heavenly fields behold,
   But must sit and mourning spin
Life's dark thread on earth below;
Let my thoughts then hourly go
Whither I myself would be,
Jesus, dearest Lord, with Thee!

J. FRANCK.

1653.

Twenty-fourth Sunday after Trinity.

Jesus answered and said unto her, Martha, Martha, thou art careful and troubled about many things: but one thing is needful, and Mary hath chosen that good part which shall not be taken away from her.

Luke x. 41, 42.

ONE thing is needful! Let me deem
   Aright of that whereof He spoke;
All else, how sweet soe'er it seem,
   Is but in truth a heavy yoke,
'Neath which the toiling spirit frets and pants,
Yet never finds the happiness it wants:
This One can make amends, whate'er I miss,
Who hath it finds in all his joy through this!

My soul, wouldst thou this one thing find?
   Seek not amid created things;
Leave what is earthly far behind,
   O'er Nature heavenward stretch thy wings,
Where God and man are One, in whom appear
All truth and fulness, thou hast found it here,—
The better part, the One thing needful He,
My One, my All, my Joy, who saveth me.

As Mary once devoutly sought
   The Eternal truth, the better part,
And sat, enwrapt in holy thought,
   At Jesu's feet with burning heart,
For nought else caring, yearning for the word
That should be spoken by her Friend, her Lord,
Losing her All in Him, His word believing,
And through the One all things again receiving:

Even so is all my heart's desire
  Fix'd, dearest Lord, on Thee alone ;
Oh make me true and draw me nigher,
  And make Thyself, O Christ, my own.
Though many turn aside to join the crowd,
To follow Thee in love my heart is vow'd,
Thy word is life and spirit, whither go ?
What joy is there in Thee we cannot know ?

All perfect wisdom lies in Thee
  As in its primal hidden source ;
Oh let my will submissive be,
  And hold henceforth its even course,
Controll'd by truth and meekness, for high Heaven
To lowly simple hearts hath wisdom given ;
Who knoweth Christ aright, and in Him lives,
Hath won the highest prize that wisdom gives.

Oh that my soul from sleep might wake,
  And ever, Lord, Thine image bear !
Thee for my portion I will take,
  Thy holiness Thou bidd'st us share,
Whate'er we need for God-like walk and life
Is given to us in Thee ; oh end this strife,
And free me from the love of passing things,
To know alone the life from Thee that springs !

What can I ask for more ? Behold
  Thy mercy is a very flood ;
I know that Thou hast pass'd of old
  Into the Holiest through Thy blood,

And there redeem'd for ever those who lay
Beneath the rule of Satan; now are they
Made free by Thee, who erst were slaves and weak,
And childlike hearts the name of Father speak.

Deep joy and peace and holy calm
   Fill my once restless spirit now;
O'er verdant pastures free from harm,
   She follows Thee, her shepherd Thou;
Whate'er rejoices or consoles us here,
Is not so sweet as feeling Thou art near;
This One is needful, but all else is dross,
Let me win Christ, all other gain is loss.

SCHRÖDER.
1697.

MARTHA

ONE THING HAVE I DESIRED
OF THE LORD, THAT WILL I SEEK AFTER; THAT
MAY DWELL IN THE HOUSE OF THE LORD ALL THE DAYS OF MY
LIFE, TO BEHOLD THE BEAUTY OF THE LORD, AND
TO ENQUIRE IN HIS TEMPLE.
Psalm xxvii. 4.

Twenty-fifth Sunday after Trinity.

Behold, the days come, saith the Lord, that I will raise unto David a righteous Branch, and a King shall reign, and prosper, and shall execute judgment and justice in the earth.

From the Passage for the Epistle.

Redeemer of the nations, come!
Ransom of earth, here make Thy home!
Bright Sun, oh dart Thy flame to earth,
For so shall God in Christ have birth!

Thou comest from Thy kingly throne,
O Son of God, the Virgin's Son!
Thou Hero of a twofold race,
Dost walk in might earth's darkest place.

Thou stoopest once to suffer here,
And risest o'er the starry sphere;
Hell's gates at Thy descent were riven,
Thy ascent is to highest Heaven.

One with the Father! Prince of might!
O'er nature's realm assert Thy right,
Our sickly bodies pine to know
Thy heavenly strength, Thy living glow.

How bright Thy lowly manger beams!
Down earth's dark vale its glory streams,
The splendour of Thy natal night
Shines through all Time in deathless light.

J. Franck.
After St. Ambrose.

ST. ANDREW'S DAY.

And Jesus saith unto them, Follow me. . . And they straightway left their nets, and followed Him.
From the Gospel.

FOLLOW me, in me ye live,
What ye ask I freely give,
Only heed ye lest ye stray,
Follow me, the Living Way;
Follow me with all your hearts,
I will ward off sorrow's darts;
Learn from Christ your Lord to be
Rich in meek humility.

Yea, Lord, meet it is indeed
We should all Thy bidding heed;
Who in fear of this world's blame,
Counts Thy lowly yoke a shame,
To Thy name, Lord, hath no right,
Is no Christian, in Thy sight.
Ah too well I know that we,
Here on earth, should follow Thee.

Where is strength, Lord, to fulfil,
Glad at heart, Thy works and will,
Following on where Thou hast trod!
All too weak am I, O God;
If awhile Thy paths I keep,
Soon I pine for rest and sleep;
E'en to love Thee, Lord, aright,
Passeth far my feeble might.

Yet I will not turn from Thee,
Yet my joy in Christ shall be;
Help me, make me strong and bold,
Firm and fast Thy grace to hold;
This world and her lusts I leave,
Only to my Lord I cleave;
All their promises are lies,
But who follows Thee is wise.

Thou hast gone before us, Lord,
Not with anger, strife, or sword,
Not with kingly pomp and pride,
But with mercy at Thy side.
Moved by wondrous love divine
For our life Thou gavest Thine,
And Thy precious outpour'd blood,
Won for us the highest good.

Let us follow in such sort,
Christ-like every deed and thought,
That Thy love most true and kind
All our hearts henceforth may bind;
None may look behind him now,
Who to Christ hath pledged his vow;
Jesus leads, no longer stand,
Follow me, is His command.

Draw me up, my God, from hence,
Raise me high o'er earth and sense,
That I lose not Thee from sight,
Nor in life nor death, my Light!
In my soul's most deep recess
Let me cherish holiness,
Not for show or human praise,
But for Thy sake, all my days.

Grant me, Lord, my heart's desire,
So my course to run nor tire,
That my practised soul may prove
What Thy meekness, what Thy love.
Grant me here to trust Thy grace,
There with joy to see Thy face,
This in time my portion be,
That through all eternity!

RIST. 1644.

St. Thomas the Apostle.

And Thomas answered and said unto Him, My Lord and my God. Jesus saith unto Him, Thomas, because thou hast seen me thou hast believed; blessed are they that have not seen, and yet have believed.

From the Gospel.

LONG in the spirit-world
    my soul had sought
Some friendly being, close to
    her akin;
Long had prepared a dwelling
    in her thought
And heart for such an one;
    for she could win
Through Him alone her
    strength, for Him she
    yearn'd,
Toward Him her fervent
    longing ever burn'd.

And rich the world in things
    invisible,
In heathen gods, and spirits
    great and small,
And bright and dark: yet
    ever did she dwell
Alone, for One was wanting
    'mid them all;

One having might and glory, rich in love,
God, who as man could shame and weakness prove.

Then came the Word, and took on Him our flesh,
   And dwelt with men, here in the world of sight,
And made an end of strife, and link'd afresh
   Our sinful earth unto the throne of light;
Into His ancient glory He is gone,
And yet He dwells with us till time be done.

Thus, O my soul, hast thou received thy will;
   The glory of the world of ghosts is dim
Before the One, who is, and was, and still
   Shall ever be; all hearts are fix'd on Him,
And spirit worlds, since He is there, become,
Hallow'd and safe to thee, thy proper home.

Thou soarest now through all their heights sublime,
   And not as once dost empty back return,
But gazing on Thy God, forgettest time
   Beneath His loving glance, whence thou wouldst learn
How thou shouldst love, and know His Word aright:
Ah, blest the love and faith that ask not sight!

PRESENTATION IN THE TEMPLE.

Lord, now lettest Thou Thy servant depart in peace, according to Thy word; for mine eyes have seen Thy salvation.

From the Gospel.

LIGHT of the Gentile world!
        Thy people's joy and love!
Drawn by Thy Spirit we are come
        Thy presence, Lord, to prove.
        Within Thy temple walls
        We wait with earnest mind,
As Simeon waited long of old
        His Saviour God to find.

        Thou wilt be found of us,
        O Lord, in every place,
Where Thou hast promised faithfully
        We should behold Thy face.
        Thou yet dost suffer us,
        Who oft are gather'd here,
To bear Thee in the arms of faith
        As once that aged seer.

        Be Thou our bliss, our light
        Shining 'mid pain and loss,
Our Sun of strength in time of fear,
        The glory round our cross;
        A glow in sinking hearts,
        A sunbeam in distress,
Physician, nurse, in sickness' hours,
        In death our happiness.

Oh let us, Lord, prevail
With Simeon at the last;
May we take up his dying song
When life is waning fast!
"Let me depart in peace,
Since that mine aged eyes
Have seen the Saviour here on earth,
Have seen His day arise."

Yes, with the eye of faith
My Jesus I behold;
No foe can rob me of my Lord,
Though fierce his threats and bold.
I dwell within Thy heart,
Thou dost in mine abide,
Not sorrow, pain nor death itself,
Can tear me from Thy side.

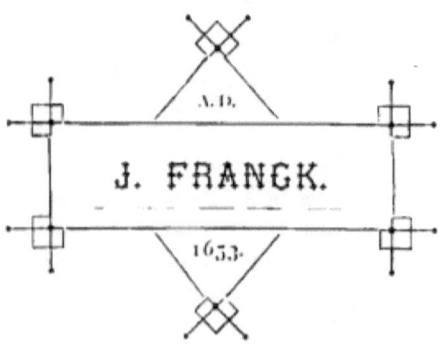

A. D.

J. FRANCK.

1653.

St. Matthias.

ST. MATTHIAS DAY

Come unto Me, all ye that labour and are heavy laden, and I will give you rest. From the Gospel.

YES, there remaineth yet a rest!
Arise, sad heart, who now dost pine,
By heavy care and pain opprest,
On whom no sun of joy can shine;
Look to the Lamb! in yon bright fields
Thou'lt know the joy His presence yields;
Cast off thy load and thither haste;
Soon shalt thou fight and bleed no more,
Soon, soon thy weary course be o'er,
And deep the rest thou then shalt taste:

The rest appointed thee of God,
The rest that nought shall break or move,
That ere this earth by man was trod
Was set apart for thee by Love.

Our Saviour gave His life to win
This rest for thee ; oh enter in !
  Hear how His voice sounds far and wide :
    Ye weary souls, no more delay,
    Nor loiter faithless by the way,
  Here in my peace and rest abide !

  Ye heavy-laden, come to Him !
    Ye who are bent with many a load,
Come from your prisons drear and dim,
    Toil not thus sadly on your road !
Ye've borne the burden of the day,
And hear ye not your Saviour say,
  I am your refuge and your rest ?
    His children ye, of heavenly birth,
    Howe'er may rage sin, hell, or earth,
  Here are ye safe, here calmly blest.

  Yonder in joy the sheaves we bring,
    Whose seed was sown on earth in tears ;
'There in our Father's house we sing
    The song too sweet for mortal ears.
Sorrow and sighing all are past,
And pain and death are fled at last,
  There with the Lamb of God we dwell,
    He leads us to the crystal river,
    He wipes away all tears for ever ;
  What there is ours no tongue can tell.

  Hunger nor thirst can pain us there,
    The time of recompense is come,

Nor cold nor scorching heat we bear,
  Safe shelter'd in our Saviour's home.
The Lamb is in the midst ; and those
Who follow'd Him through shame and woes,
  Are crown'd with honour, joy, and peace.
    The dry bones gather life again,
    One Sabbath over all shall reign,
Wherein all toil and labour cease.

There is untroubled calm and light,
  No gnawing care shall mar our rest ;
Ye weary, heed this word aright,
  Come, lean upon your Saviour's breast.
Fain would I linger here no more,
Fain to yon happier world upsoar,
  And join that bright expectant band.
    Oh raise, my soul, the joyful song
    That rings through yon triumphant throng ;
Thy perfect rest is nigh at hand.

KUNTH.

1733.

The Annunciation.

Behold the handmaid of the Lord; be it unto me according to Thy word.
From the Gospel.

Oh my spirit fain would sink
   In Thy heart and hands, my God,
Waiting till Thou show the end
   Of the ways she here hath trod ;
Stripp'd of self, how calm her rest
On her loving Father's breast !

And my soul repineth not,
   Well content whate'er befall ;
Murmurs, wishes, of self-will,
   They are slain and vanquish'd all,
Restless thoughts, that fret and crave,
Slumber in her Saviour's grave.

And my soul is free from care,
   For her thoughts from all things cease
That can pierce like sharpest thorns
   Wounding sore the inner peace.
He who made her careth well,
She but seeks in peace to dwell.

And my soul despaireth not,
   Loving God amid her woe ;
Grief that wrings and breaks the heart
   Only they who hate Him know :
They who love Him still possess
Comfort in their worst distress.

And my soul complaineth not,
  For she knows not pain or fear,
Clinging to her God in faith,
  Trusting though He slay her here.
'Tis when flesh and blood repine,
Sun of joy, Thou canst not shine.

Thus my soul before her God
  Lieth still, nor speaketh more,
Conqueror thus o'er pain and wrong,
  That once smote her to the core ;
Like a silent ocean, bright
With her God's great praise and light.

WINKLER.

1713.

NOT·OF·BLOOD·NOR·OF·THE·WILL·OF·THE·FLESH.
NOR·OF·THE·WILL·OF·MAN·
BUT·OF·GOD.

St. Barnabas' Day.

We preach unto you that ye should turn from these vanities unto the living God which made heaven, and earth, and the sea, and all things that are therein: who in time past suffered all nations to walk in their own ways. Nevertheless He left not Himself without witness, in that He did good, and gave us rain from heaven, and fruitful seasons, filling our hearts with food and gladness.

From the Lesson.

SHALL I not sing praise to Thee,

Shall I not give thanks, O Lord ?

Since for us in all I see

How Thou keepest watch and ward ;

How the truest tenderest love

Ever fills Thy heart, my God,

Helping, cheering, on their road,

All who in Thy service move.

All things else have but their day,

God's love only lasts for aye.

As the eagle o'er her nest
  Spreads her sheltering wings abroad,
So from all that would molest,
  Doth Thine arm defend me, Lord ;
From my youth up e'en till now
  Of the being Thou didst give,
  And the earthly life I live,
Faithful Guardian still wert Thou.
          All things else have but their day,
          God's love only lasts for aye.

Nay, He kept not back His Son,
  But hath given Him for our good,
And our safety He hath won
  By the shedding of His blood.
O Thou fathomless abyss !
  My weak powers but strive in vain,
  Knowledge of Thy depths to gain,
Man knows not such love as this.
          All things else have but their day,
          God's love only lasts for aye.

And His Spirit, blessed Guide,
  In His holy Word doth teach,
How on earth we may abide,
  So that heaven at last we reach ;
Every longing heart doth fill
  With the pure true light of faith,
  That can break the bonds of death,
And control the powers of ill.
          All things else have but their day,
          God's love only lasts for aye.

Truly hath He cared indeed
  For my soul's health, and no less
If my body suffer need,
  Will He help in my distress.
When my strength and courage fail,
  When my powers can do no more,
  Doth my God such strength outpour,
That I rise up and prevail.
      All things else have but their day,
      God's love only lasts for aye.

All the hosts of heaven and earth,
  Hath He placed at my command,
Nowhere is there lack or dearth,
  But I find in sea and land
All things order'd for my wants,
  Living things in fields and woods,
  On the heights or in the floods,
And the earth brings forth her plants.
      All things else have but their day,
      God's love only lasts for aye.

When I sleep my Guardian wakes,
  And revives my wearied mind ;
Every morning on me breaks
  With some mark of love most kind ;
Had my God not stood my Friend,
  Had His countenance not been
  Here my guide, I had not seen
Many a trial reach its end.
      All things else have but their day,
      God's love only lasts for aye.

Often hath my crafty Foe
  Threaten'd to bring down on me
Many a sore and heavy woe,
  From which yet my life is free;
For the angel whom God sends,
  Wards off every threaten'd hurt,
  Every evil doth avert
That mine Enemy intends.
      All things else have but their day,
      God's love only lasts for aye.

As a father ne'er withdraws
  From a child his all of love,
Though it often break his laws,
  Though it careless, wilful, prove:
Even so my loving Lord
  Doth my faults with pity see,
  With His rod He chastens me,
Not avenging with His sword.
      All things else have but their day,
      God's love only lasts for aye.

When His strokes upon me light,
  Bitterly I feel their smart,
Yet are they, if seen aright,
  Tokens that my Father's heart
Yearns to bring me back again
  Through these crosses to His fold,
  From the world that fain would hold
Soul and body in its chain.
      All things else have but their day,
      God's love only lasts for aye.

All my life I still have found,
  And I will forget it never,
Every sorrow hath its bound,
  And no cross endures for ever.
After all the winter's snows
  Comes sweet summer back again,
  Patient souls ne'er wait in vain,
Joy is given for all their woes.
      All things else have but their day,
      God's love only lasts for aye.

Since then neither change nor end
  In Thy love can e'er have place,
Father! I beseech Thee send
  Unto me Thy loving grace.
Help Thy feeble child, and give
  Strength to serve Thee day and night,
  Loving Thee with all my might,
While on earth I yet must live;
      So shall I when Time is o'er,
      Praise and love Thee evermore.

PAUL GERHARDT.
1659.

ST. MICHAEL
AND ALL ANGELS.

PRAISE and thanks to Thee be sung,
   Mighty God, in sweetest tone !
Lo ! from every land and tongue,
   Nations gather round Thy Throne,
Praising Thee, that Thou dost send,
   Daily from Thy Heaven above,
   Angel-messengers of love,
Who Thy threaten'd Church defend.
Who can offer worthily,
Lord of angels, praise to Thee !

'Tis your office, Spirits bright,
   Still to guard us night and day,
And before your heavenly might,
   Powers of darkness flee away ;
Ever doth your unseen host
   Camp around us, and avert
   All that seeks to do us hurt,
Curbing Satan's malice most.
Lord, who then can worthily
For such goodness honour Thee !

And ye come on ready wing,
   When we drift toward sheer despair,
Seeing nought where we might cling,
   Suddenly, lo, ye are there !
And the wearied heart grows strong.

ARE THEY NOT ALL MINISTERING SPIRITS, SENT FORTH TO MINISTER FOR THEM THAT SHALL BE HEIRS OF SALVATION ? Heb. i. 14.

As an angel strengthen'd Him,
Fainting in the garden dim,
'Neath the world's vast woe and wrong.
Lord, who then can worthily
For such mercy honour Thee !

Right and seemly is it then
  We should glory, that our God
Hath such honour put on men,
  That He sends o'er earth abroad
Princes of the realm above,
  Champions, who by day and night,
  Shield us with His holy might ;
Come, behold how great His love !
Lord, who then can worthily
For such favour honour Thee !

Praise and thanks to Thee be sung,
  Mighty God, in sweetest tone.
Lo ! from every land and tongue,
  Nations gather round Thy throne,
Praising Thee that Thou dost send,
  Hourly from Thy glorious sphere,
  Angels down to help us here,
And Thy threaten'd Church defend.
Let us henceforth worthily,
Lord of angels, honour Thee.

RIST.
1655.

All Saints Day

*Lo, a great multitude which no man
could number, of all nations, and
kindreds, and people, and tongues,
stood before the throne and before the
Lamb, clothed with white robes, and
palms in their hands; and cried
with a loud voice, saying, Salvation
to our God which sitteth upon the
throne and unto the Lamb.*

From the Epistle.

WhO are those before God's throne,
　　What the crownèd host I see?
As the sky with stars thick-strown
　　Is their shining company:
Hallelujahs, hark, they sing,
Solemn praise to God they bring.

Who are those that in their hands
　　Bear aloft the conqueror's palm,
As one o'er his foeman stands,
　　Fallen beneath his mighty arm?
What the war and what the strife,
　　Whence came such victorious life?

Who are those array'd in light,
　　Cloth'd in righteousness divine,
Wearing robes most pure and white,
　　That unstain'd shall ever shine,
That can nevermore decay;
　　Whence came all this bright array?

They are those who, strong in faith,
 Battled for the mighty God ;
Conquerors o'er the world and death,
 Following not Sin's crowded road ;
Through the Lamb who once was slain,
Did they such high victory gain.

They are those who much have borne,
 Trial, sorrow, pain, and care,
Who have wrestled night and morn
 With the mighty God in prayer ;
Now their strife hath found its close,
God hath turn'd away their woes.

They are branches of that Stem,
 Who hath our Salvation been,
In the blood He shed for them,
 Have they made their raiment clean ;
Hence they wear such radiant dress,
Clad in spotless holiness.

They are those who hourly here
 Served as priests before their Lord,
Offering up with gladsome cheer
 Soul and body at His word.
Now within the Holy Place,
They behold Him face to face.

As the harts at noonday pant
 For the river fresh and clear,
Did they ofttimes long and faint
 For the Living Fountain here.
Now their thirst is quench'd, they dwell
With the Lord they loved so well.

Thitherwards I stretch my hands;
  O Lord Jesus, day by day,
In Thy house in these strange lands,
  Compass'd round with foes, I pray,
Let me sink not in the war,
Drive for me my foes afar.

Cast my lot in earth and heaven
  With Thy saints made like to Thee,
Let my bonds be also riven,
  Make Thy child who loves Thee free;
Near the throne where Thou dost shine,
May a place at last be mine!

Ah! that bliss can ne'er be told,
  When with all that army bright,
Thee, my Sun, I shall behold,
  Shining star-like, with Thy light.
Amen! Thanks be brought to Thee,
Praise through all eternity.

SCHENK.

DIED
1727.

Morning Hymns

Morning Hymns.

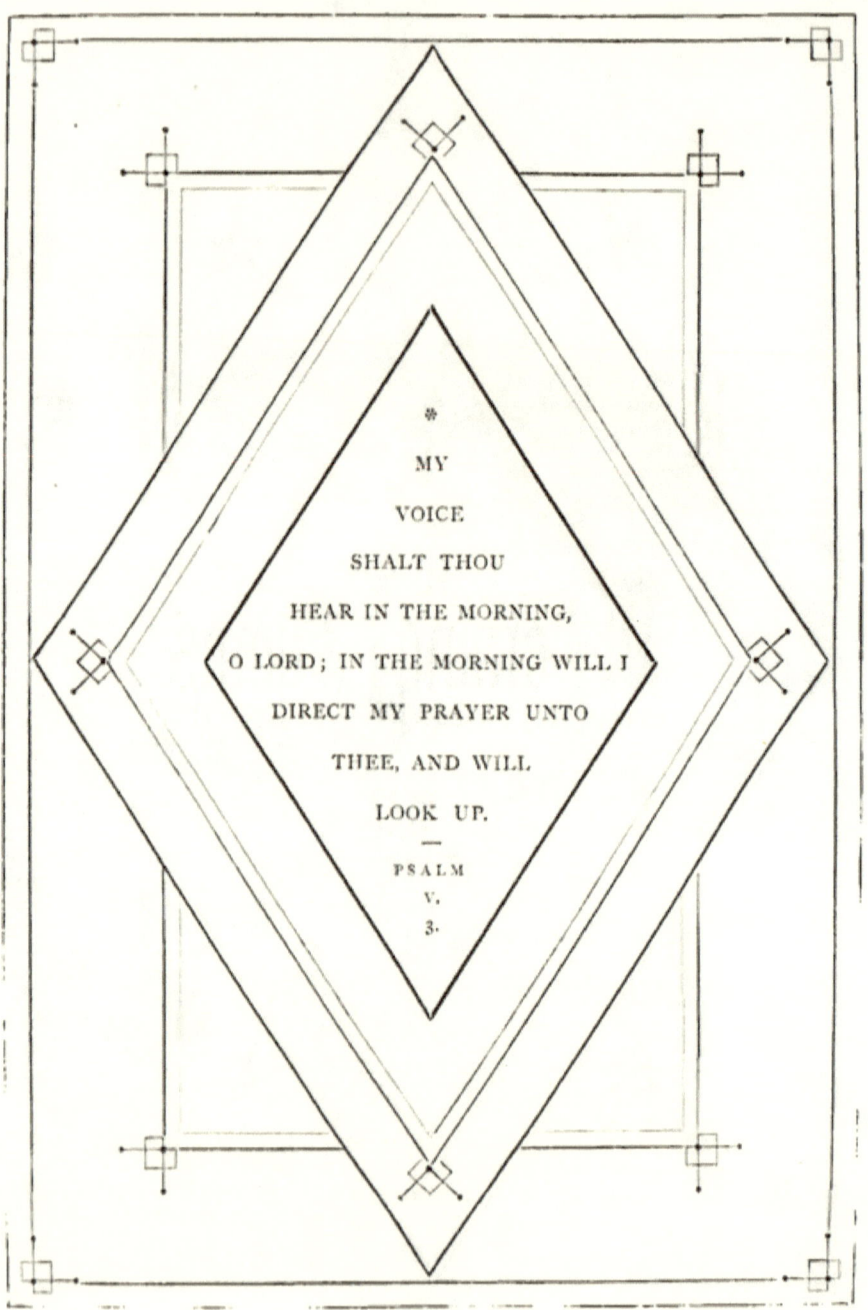

*

MY

VOICE

SHALT THOU

HEAR IN THE MORNING,

O LORD; IN THE MORNING WILL I

DIRECT MY PRAYER UNTO

THEE, AND WILL

LOOK UP.

—

PSALM

V.

3.

Morning Hymns.

I.

GOD who madest earth and heaven,
    Father, Son, and Holy Ghost,
Who the day and night hast given,
    Sun and moon and starry host,
All things wake at Thy command,
Held in being by Thy hand :

God, I thank Thee from my heart,
    That through all the livelong night,
Thou hast kept me safe apart
    From all danger, pain, affright,
And the cunning of my foe
Hath not wrought my overthrow.

Let the night of sin depart,
    As this earthly night hath fled ;
Jesus, take me to Thy heart,
    In the blood that Thou hast shed
Is my help and hope alone,
For the evil I have done.

Help me as each morn shall break,
  In the Spirit to arise,
Let my soul from sin awake,
  That when o'er the aged skies,
Shall the morn of Doom appear,
I may see it free from fear.

Ever lead me, ever guide
  All my wanderings by Thy Word;
As Thou hast been, still abide
  My defence, my refuge, Lord.
Never safe except with Thee,
Ever Thou my Guardian be!

Mighty God, I now commend
  Soul and body unto Thee,
All the powers that Thou dost lend,
  By Thy hand directed be;
Thou my boast, my strength divine,
Keep me with Thee, I am Thine.

Let Thine angel guard my soul
  From the Evil One's dark power,
All his thousand wiles control,
  Warning, guiding me each hour,
Till my final rest be come,
And Thine angel bear me home.

HEINRICH ALBERT.

1644.

II.

THE golden sunbeams with their joyous gleams,
    Are kindling o'er earth, her life and mirth,
Shedding forth lovely and heart-cheering light ;
    Through the dark hours' chill I lay silent
        and still,
    But risen at length to gladness and strength,
    I gaze on the heavens all glowing and bright.

    Mine eyes now behold Thy works, that of old
    And ever are telling to all men here dwelling,
How great is Thy glory, how wondrous Thy power ;
    They tell of the home where the faithful shall come,
    Who depart to that peace that can change not or cease,
From earth where all passeth as passes the hour.

    O come let us raise our voices, and praise
    The Maker of all, at His feet let us fall,
Offering to Him again all He hath given,
    The best that is ours, our hearts and our powers ;
    Glad songs that we sing Him, thanks that we bring Him,
These are the incense most grateful to Heaven.

    Evening and morning thus ever He cares for us,
    Blessing, renewing, warding off ruin,
These are His works, thus His goodness we prove ;

When we are sleeping, watch He is keeping,
  When we arise, He gladdens our eyes
With the sunshine of mercy, the glow of His love.

All passeth away, but God liveth aye,
  And changeth in nought ; eternal His Thought,
His Word and His Will are steadfast and sure ;
  Never His grace nor His mercy decays,
  It heals the sad heart from its deadliest smart,
Giving it life that shall ever endure.

God, Thou my crown ! forgiving look down,
  And hide from Thy face through Thy pitying grace,
All my transgressions against Thy command ;
  Henceforth oh rule me, guide me and school me,
  As Thou seest fit ; my ways I commit
All to Thy pleasure, Thy merciful hand.

Crosses and sorrow may end with the morrow,
  Stormiest seas shall sink into peace,
The wild winds are hush'd, and the sunshine returns :
  So fulness of rest, and the calm of the blest,
  Are waiting me there, in that garden most fair,
That home for which daily my spirit here yearns.

PAUL GERHARDT.

III.

COME, my soul, awake, 'tis morning,
    Day is dawning
O'er the earth, arise and pray;
    Come, to Him who made this splendour,
    Thou must render
All thy feeble powers can pay.

From the stars now learn thy duty,
    See their beauty
Paling in the golden air;
So God's light thy mists should banish,
    Thus should vanish
What to darken'd sense seem'd fair.

See how everything that liveth,
    Gladly striveth
On the pleasant light to gaze;
Stirs with joy each thing that groweth,
    As it knoweth
Darkness smitten by these rays.

Soul, thy incense also proffer ;
 Thou shouldst offer
Praise to Him, who from thy head
Kept afar the storms of sorrow,
 And the morrow
Finds the night in peace hath fled.

Bid Him bless what thou art doing,
 If pursuing
Some good aim ; but if there lurks
Ill intent in thine endeavour,
 May He ever
Thwart and turn thee from thy works.

Think that He, the All-discerning,
 Knows each turning
Of thy path, each sinful stain ;
Nay what shame would fain gloss over,
 Can discover ;
All thou dost to Him is plain.

Bound unto the flying hours
 Are our powers ;
Earth's vain good floats down their wave.
That thy ship, my soul, is hasting,
 Never resting,
To its haven in the grave.

Pray that when thy life is closing,
    Calm reposing,
Thou mayst die, and not in pain ;
That, the night of death departed,
    Thou glad-hearted,
Mayst behold the Sun again,

From God's glances shrink thou never,
    Meet them ever ;
Who submits him to His grace,
Finds that earth no sunshine knoweth
    Such as gloweth
O'er his pathway all his days.

Wakenest thou again to sorrow,
    Oh ! then borrow
Strength from Him, whose sun-like might
On the mountain-summit tarries,
    And yet carries
To the vales their mirth and light.

Round the gifts He on thee showers,
    Fiery towers
Will He set, be not afraid,
Thou shalt dwell 'mid angel legions,
    In the regions
Satan's self dares not invade.

VON CANITZ. 1654-1699.

IV.

AYSPRING of Eternity !
Dawn on us this morning-tide.
Light from Light's exhaustless sea,
Now no more Thy radiance hide,
But dispel with glorious might
All our night.

Let the morning dew of love
On our sleeping conscience rain ;
Gentle comfort from above
Flow through life's long parchèd plain ;
Water daily us Thy flock
From the rock.

Let the glow of love destroy
Cold obedience faintly given ;
Wake our hearts to strength and joy
With the flushing eastern heaven,
Let us truly rise ere yet
Life hath set.

Brightest Star of eastern skies,
 Let that final morn appear,
When our bodies too shall rise
 Free from all that pain'd them here,
Strong their joyful course to run
  As the sun.

To yon world be Thou our light,
 O Thou glorious Sun of grace ;
Lead us through the tearful night,
 To yon fair and blessed place,
Where to joy that never dies
  We shall rise.

Von Rosenroth.
1684.

V.

NCE more from rest I rise again,
To greet a day of toil and pain,
 My Heaven-appointed lot :
Unknowing what new grief may be
With this new day in store for me.
But it shall harm me not
I know full well ; my loving God
Will send me not a hurtful load.

My burden every day is new,
But every day my God is true.
 And all my cares hath borne :
Ere eventide can no man know

What Day shall bring of joy or woe,
　And though it seem each morn
To some new path of suffering call,
With God I can surmount it all.

Since this I know, oh wherefore sink,
My faithless heart? And why thus shrink
　　To take thy load again?
Bear what thou canst, God bears thy lot,
The Lord of All, He stumbleth not;
　　Pure blessing shalt thou gain,
If thou with Him right onward go,
Nor fear'st to tread the path of woe.

My heart grows strong, all terrors fly
Whene'er I feel Thy love Most High,
　　Doth compass me around;
But would I have Thee for my shield,
No more to sin my soul must yield,
　　But in Thy ways be found;
Thou, God, wilt never walk my way
If from Thy paths my feet should stray.

But let me feel Thou guidest me,
And humbly I will follow Thee,
　　Lord, make me true and pure;
Then strong and dauntless in Thy might
Against a world of sin I'll fight,
　　And know my triumph sure;

Then bravely I can meet each day,
And fear it not, come what come may.

My God and Lord, I cast on Thee
The load that weighs too sore on me,
    The yoke 'neath which I bow;
I lay my rank, my high command,
In my Almighty Father's hand,
    Well knowing, Lord, that Thou
Wilt ne'er withdraw it, for Thy truth
Hath led me onward from my youth.

To Thee my kindred I commend,
For they are safe if Thou defend,
    Oh guard them round about;
My sinful soul would shelter take
In Jesu's bosom, for whose sake
    Thou wilt not cast her out;
When soul and body part at last,
Then all myself on Thee I cast.

ANTON ULRICH,

Duke of Brunswick.

1767.

Evening Hymns.

Evening Hymns.

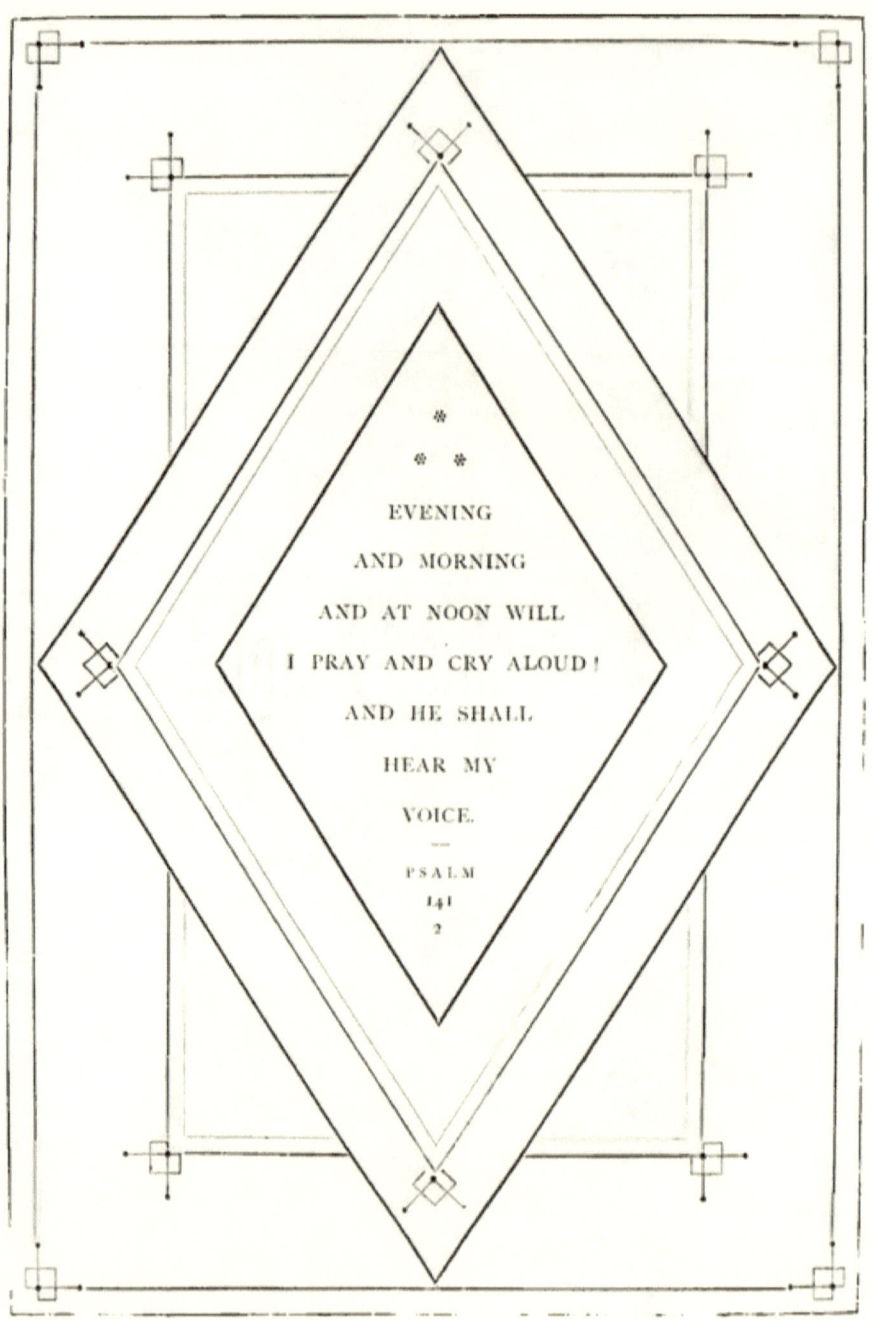

EVENING

AND MORNING

AND AT NOON WILL

I PRAY AND CRY ALOUD!

AND HE SHALL

HEAR MY

VOICE.

PSALM
141
2

Evening Hymns.

I.

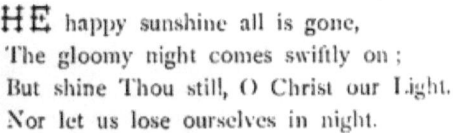

HE happy sunshine all is gone,
The gloomy night comes swiftly on;
But shine Thou still, O Christ our Light,
Nor let us lose ourselves in night.

We thank Thee, Father, that this day
Thy angels watch'd around our way,
And free from harm and vexing fear,
Have led us on in safety here.

Lord, have we anger'd Thee to-day,
Remember not our sins, we pray,
But let Thy mercy o'er them sweep,
And give us calm and restful sleep.

Thy angels guard our sleeping hours,
And keep afar all evil Powers;
And Thou all pain and mischief ward
From soul and body, faithful Lord!

N. Hermann.

1560.

II.

NOW all the woods are sleeping,
 And night and stillness creeping
O'er field and city, man and beast;
 But thou, my heart, awake thee,
 To prayer awhile betake thee,
And praise thy Maker ere thou rest.

 O Sun, where art thou vanish'd!
 The Night thy reign hath banish'd,
Thy ancient foe, the Night.
 Farewell, a brighter glory
 My Jesus sheddeth o'er me,
All clear within me shines His light.

 The last faint beam is going,
 The golden stars are glowing
In yonder dark-blue deep:
 And such the glory given
 When called of God to heaven.
On earth no more we pine and weep.

 The body hastes to slumber,
 These garments now but cumber;
And as I lay them by
 I ponder how the spirit
 Puts off the flesh t' inherit
A shining robe with Christ on high.

Now thought and labour ceases,
For Night the tired releases
And bids sweet rest begin :
My heart, there comes a morrow
Shall set thee free from sorrow
And all the dreary toil of sin.

Ye aching limbs ! now rest you,
For toil hath sore oppress'd you,
Lie down my weary head :
A sleep shall once o'ertake you
From which earth ne'er shall wake you,
Within a narrower colder bed.

My heavy eyes are closing,
When I lie deep reposing—
O soul and body, where are ye !
To helpless sleep I yield them,
Oh let Thy mercy shield them,
Thou sleepless Eye, their guardian be :

My Jesus, stay Thou by me,
And let no foe come nigh me,
Safe shelter'd by Thy wing ;
But would the foe alarm me,
Oh let him never harm me,
But still Thine angels round me sing !

My loved ones, rest securely,
From every peril surely
Our God will guard your heads ;
And happy slumbers send you,
And bid His hosts attend you,
And golden-arm'd watch o'er your beds.

PAUL GERHARDT.

1653.

III.

THE day expires ;
My soul desires
And pants to see that day,
When the vexing cares of earth
Shall be done away.

The night is here ;
Oh ! be Thou near,
Christ, make it light within ;
Drive away from out my heart
All the night of sin.

The sunbeams pale,
And flee and fail ;
O uncreated Sun !
Let Thy light now shine on us,
Then our joy were won.

All things that move
Below, above,
Now with sleep are blest;
Work Thou still in me, while I
Calmly in Thee rest.

When shall the sway
Of night and day
Cease to rule man thus?
When that brightest day of days
Once shall dawn on us.

Ah! never then
Her light again
Jerusalem shall miss,
For the Lamb shall be her Light,
Filling her with bliss.

Oh were I there!
Where all the air
With lovely sounds is ringing;
Where the saints Thee, Holy Lord,
Evermore are singing!

Lord Jesus, Thou
My rest art now,
Oh help me that I come,
Radiant with Thy light to shine
In Thy glorious home!

FREYLINGHAUSEN.

1704.

IV.

THE moon hath risen on high,
And in the clear dark sky
The golden stars all brightly glow;
   And black and hush'd the woods,
While o'er the fields and floods
The white mists hover to and fro.

   How still the earth! how calm!
   What dear and home-like charm
From gentle twilight doth she borrow!
   Like to some quiet room,
   Where wrapt in still soft gloom,
We sleep away the daylight's sorrow.

   Look up; the moon to-night
   Shows us but half her light,
And yet we know her round and fair.
   At other things how oft
   We in our blindness scoff'd,
Because we saw not what was there.

   We haughty sons of men
   Have but a narrow ken,
We are but sinners poor and weak.
   Yet airy dreams we build,
   And deem us wise and skill'd,
And come not nearer what we seek.

Thy mercy let us see,
Nor find in vanity
Our joy; nor trust in what departs;
But true and simple grow,
And live to Thee below
With sunny pure and childlike hearts.

Let Death all gently come
At last to take us home,
And let us meet him fearlessly;
And when these bonds are riven,
Oh take us to Thy heaven,
Our Lord and God, to dwell with Thee.

Now in His name most blest
My brethren sink to rest;
The wind is cold, chill falls the dew.
Spare us, O God, and keep
Us safe in quiet sleep,
And all the sick and suffering too.

CLAUDIUS.

1782.

* * * *
* *
*
*

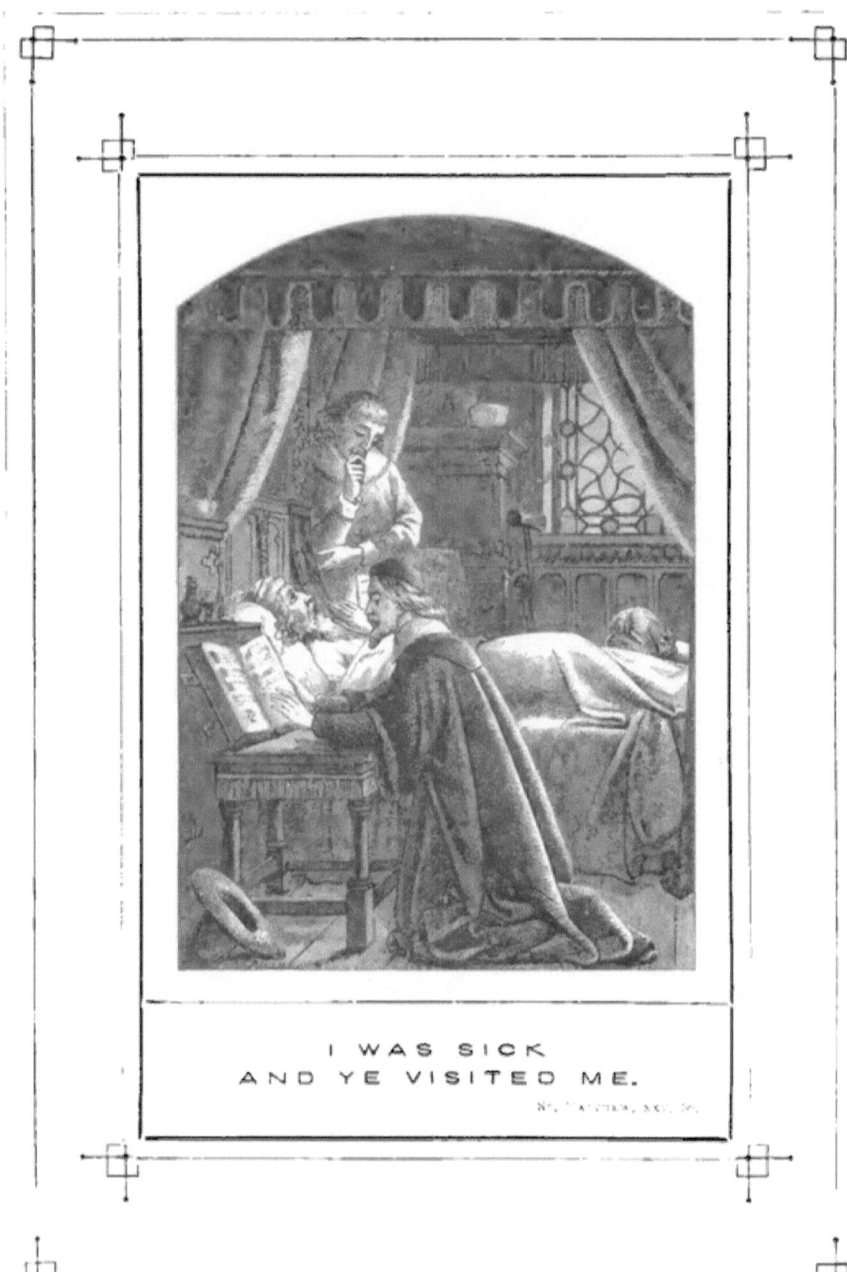

I WAS SICK
AND YE VISITED ME.

for the

Sick & Dying

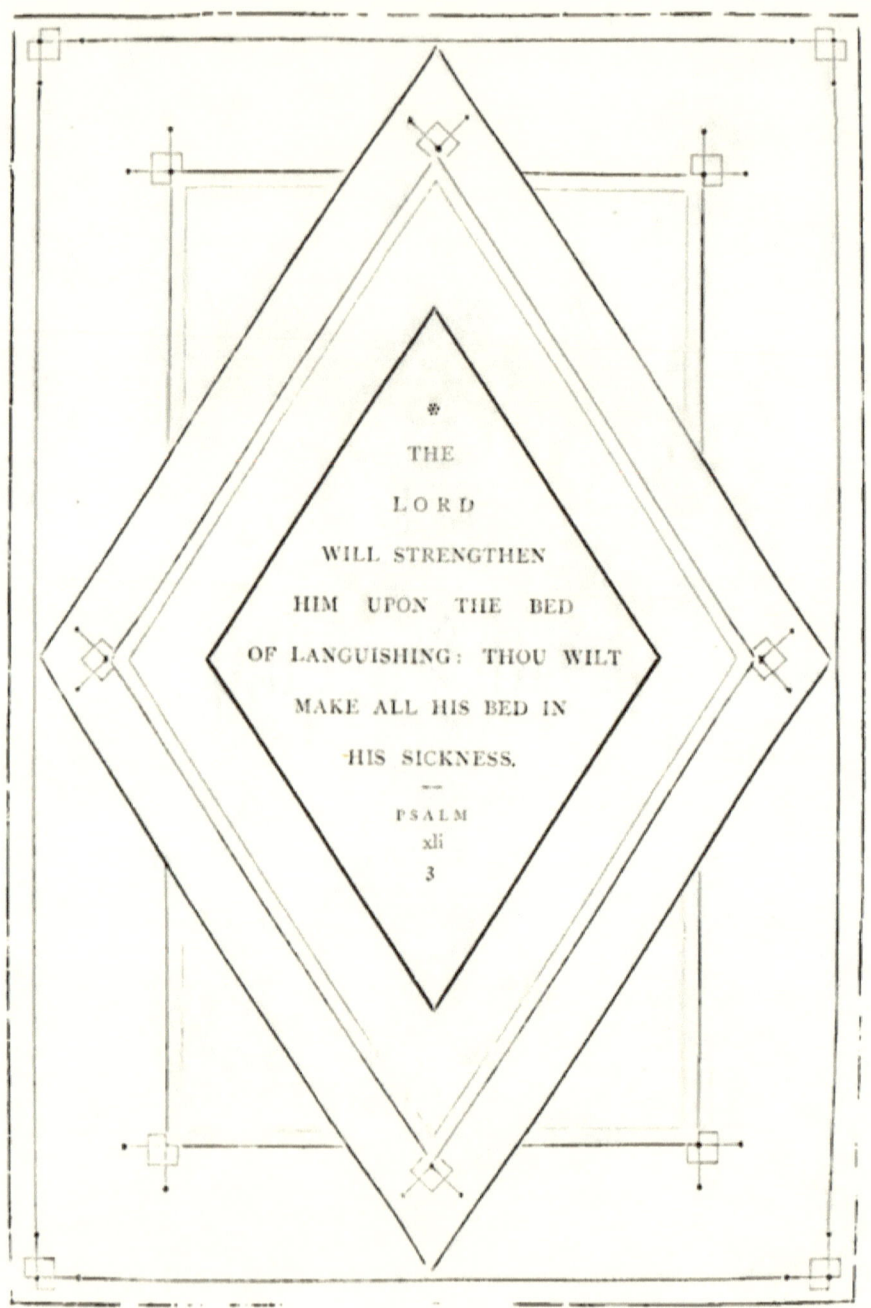

THE
LORD
WILL STRENGTHEN
HIM UPON THE BED
OF LANGUISHING: THOU WILT
MAKE ALL HIS BED IN
HIS SICKNESS.

PSALM
xli
3

HYMNS
FOR THE SICK
AND DYING.

I.

IN the midst of life, behold
 Death has girt us round.
Whom for help then shall we pray,
 Where shall grace be found?
In Thee, O Lord, alone!
 We rue the evil we have done,
 That Thy wrath on us hath drawn.
  Holy Lord and God!
  Strong and Holy God!
Merciful and Holy Saviour!
 Eternal God!
Leave us not to sink beneath
These dark pains of bitter death;
 Kyrie eleison!

In the midst of death the jaws
 Of hell against us gape.
Who from peril dire as this
 Openeth us escape?

'Tis Thou, O Lord, alone !
   Our bitter suffering and our sin
   Pity from Thy mercy win,
      Holy Lord and **God** !
      Strong and Holy God !
   Merciful and Holy Saviour !
      Eternal God !
   Let **not** dread our souls o'erwhelm
   Of **the dark** and burning realm,
      Kyrie eleison !

In the midst of hell would Sin
   Drive us to despair ;
Whither shall we flee away ?
   Where is refuge, where ?
With Thee, Lord Christ, alone !
   For Thou hast shed Thy precious blood,
All our sins Thou makest good,
   Holy Lord and God !
   Strong and holy God !
Merciful and holy Saviour !
   Eternal God !
Leave us not to fall in death
From the hope of Thy true Faith,
   Kyrie eleison !

NOTKER,
   Trans. by LUTHER.
      Written about 900.
         Tr. 1524.

246

II.

GOD whom I as love have known,
  Thou hast sickness laid on me,
  And these pains are sent of Thee,
  Under which I burn and moan ;
  Let them burn away the sin,
That too oft hath check'd the love
Wherewith Thou my heart wouldst move,
When Thy Spirit works within !

In my weakness be Thou strong,
  Be Thou sweet when I am sad,
  Let me still in Thee be glad,
Though my pains be keen and long.
All that plagues my body now,
  All that wasteth me away,
  Pressing on me night and day,
Love ordains, for Love art Thou !

Suffering is the work now sent,
  Nothing can I do but lie
  Suffering as the hours go by ;
All my powers to this are bent.
Suffering is my gain ; I bow
  To my heavenly Father's will,
  And receive it hush'd and still ;
Suffering is my worship now.

God ! I take it from Thy hand
  As a sign of love, I know
  Thou wouldst perfect me through woe,
Till I pure before Thee stand.

All refreshment, all the food
   Given me for the body's need,
   Comes from Thee, who lov'st indeed,
Comes from Thee, for Thou art good.

Let my soul beneath her load
   Faint not, through the o'erwearied flesh ;
   Let her hourly drink afresh
Love and peace from Thee, my God.
Let the body's pain and smart
   Hinder not her flight to Thee,
   Nor the calm Thou givest me ;
Keep Thou up the sinking heart.

Grant me never to complain,
   Make me to Thy will resign'd,
   With a quiet, humble mind,
Cheerful on my bed of pain.
In the flesh who suffers thus,
   Shall be purified from sin,
   And the soul renew'd within :
Therefore pain is laid on us.

I commend to Thee my life,
   And my body to the cross ;
   Never let me think it loss
That I thus am freed from strife—
Wholly Thine ; my faith is sure
   Whether life or death be mine,
   I am safe if I am Thine ;
For 'tis Love that makes me pure.

                RICHTER. 1713.

III.

WHEN the last agony draws nigh,
My spirit sinks in bitter fear:
Courage! I conquer though I die,
For Christ with Death once wrestled here.
Thy strife, O Christ, with Death's dark power
Upholds me in this fearful hour.

In faith I hide myself in Thee,
I shall not perish in the strife;
I share Thy war, Thy victory,
And Death is swallow'd up in Life.
Thy strife, O Christ, with Death of yore
Hath conquer'd, and I fear no more.

ANON.

IV.

LORD Jesus Christ, true Man and God,
Who borest anguish, scorn, the rod,
And diedst at last upon the tree,
To bring Thy Father's grace to me:
I pray Thee through that bitter woe,
Let me, a sinner, mercy know.

When comes the hour of failing breath,
And I must wrestle, Lord, with death,
When from my sight all fades away,
And when my tongue no more can say,
And when mine ears no more can hear,
And when my heart is rack'd with fear ;

When all my mind is darken'd o'er,
And human help can do no more,
Then come, Lord Jesus, come with speed,
And help me in my hour of need,
Lead me from this dark vale beneath,
And shorten then the pangs of death.

All evil spirits drive away,
But let Thy Spirit with me stay
Until my soul the body leave ;
Then in Thy hands my soul receive,
And let the earth my body keep,
Till the Last Day shall break its sleep.

Joyful my resurrection be,
Thou in the Judgment plead for me,
And hide my sins, Lord, from Thy face,
And give me Life of Thy dear grace !
I trust Thee utterly, my Lord,
For Thou hast promised in Thy Word :

"In truth I tell you, who receives
My word, and keeps it, and believes,
Shall never fall God's wrath beneath,
Shall never taste eternal death ;
Though here on earth, in time, he die,
He is not therefore lost ; for I

Will come, and with a mighty hand
Will break away Death's strongest band,
And lift him hence that he shall be
For ever in my realm with Me,
For ever living there in bliss."
Ah let us not that glory miss !

Dear Lord, forgive us all our guilt,
Help us to wait until Thou wilt
That we depart ; and let our faith
Be brave and conquer e'en in death,
Firm resting on Thy sacred Word,
Until we sleep in Thee, our Lord.

PAUL EBER.

1557.

V.

GO and dig my grave to-day!
    Weary of my wanderings all,
Now from earth I pass away,
    For the heavenly peace doth call;
Angel voices from above
Call me to their rest and love.

Go and dig my grave to-day!
    Homeward doth my journey tend,
And I lay my staff away
    Here where all things earthly end,
And I lay my weary head
In the only painless bed.

What is there I yet should do,
    Lingering in this darksome vale?
Proud and mighty, fair to view,
    Are our schemes, and yet they fail,
Like the sand before the wind,
That no power of man can bind.

Farewell, earth, then; I am glad
    That in peace I now depart,
For thy very joys are sad,
    And thy hopes deceive the heart;
Fleeting is thy beauty's gleam,
False and changing as a dream.

And to you a last good night,
   Sun and moon and stars so dear ;
Farewell all your golden light ;
   I am travelling far from here,
To the splendours of that day
Where ye all must fade away.

Farewell, O ye much-loved friends !
   Grief hath smote you as a sword,
But the Comforter descends
   Unto them who love the Lord.
Weep not o'er a passing show,
To th' eternal world I go.

Weep not that I take my leave
   Of the world ; that I exchange
Errors that too closely cleave,
   Shadows, empty ghosts that range
Through this world of nought and night,
For a land of truth and light.

Weep not, dearest to my heart,
   For I find my Saviour near,
And I know that I have part
   In the pains He suffer'd here,
When He shed His sacred blood
For the whole world's highest good.

Weep not, my Redeemer lives ;
   Heavenward springing from the dust.
Clear-eyed Hope her comfort gives ;

Faith, Heaven's champion, bids us trust ;
Love eternal whispers nigh,
"Child of God, fear not to die !"

E. M. ARNDT.

VI.

HEN I have conquer'd ; then at last
My course is run, good night !
I am well pleased that it is past ;
A thousand times, good night !
But ye, dear friends, whom I must leave,
Look not thus anxiously ;
O wherefore thus lament and grieve ?
It standeth well with me.

Farewell, O anguish, pain, and fear,
Farewell, farewell for ever !
It glads my heart to leave you here,
Redeem'd from you for ever !
Henceforth a life of joy I share,
In my Creator's hand ;
None of the griefs can touch me there,
That haunt this lower land.

Who yet o'er earth in time must roam,
Not yet from error free,
Scarce lisp the language of our home,
The glad eternity.

Far better is a happy death,
  Than worldly life, I trow ;
The weakness once I sank beneath,
  I nevermore shall know.

Lay on my coffin many a wreath,
  For conquerors wreath'd are seen ;
And lo ! my soul attains through death
  The crown of evergreen,
That blooms in fadeless groves of heaven ;
  And this fair victor's crown,
That mighty Son of God hath given,
  Who for my sake came down.

'Twas but a while that I was sent
  To dwell among you here ;
Now God resumes what He hath lent,
  Oh grieve not o'er my bier ;
But say, 'twas given at His command
  Who takes it, He is just ;
Our life and death are in His hand,
  His servants can but trust.

That ye should see my grave, alas !
  Shows we are frail indeed ;
That it so soon should come to pass.
  Our Father hath decreed,
And He your bitter grief shall still ;
  Think not too young am I,
For he who dies as God doth will,
  Is old enough to die.

Farewell, thou dear, dear soul, farewell!
  To those sweet pleasures go,
That we who mourning here must dwell,
  Not yet, alas! can know.
Ah when shall that great day be come,
  When these things fade away,
And Thou shalt bid us welcome home;
  Would God it were to-day!

SACER.

1665.

VII.

 Y God, to Thee I now commend
  My soul; for Thou, O Lord,
Dost live and love me without end,
  And wilt perform Thy word.

To whom else should I make my plea,
  That heavenly life be mine?
All souls, my God, belong to Thee,
  My soul is also Thine.

Thou gav'st my spirit at my birth,
  Take back what Thou hast given;
And with the Lord I served on earth,
  Grant me to live in heaven.

LYRA GERMANICA.

Faith spreads her wings, she sees reveal'd
  The shining walls above;
My spirit knows that she is seal'd,
  Redeem'd from death by love.

Thou my Deliverer wast of yore,
  From sin Thou mad'st me free,
Now, faithful God, dost Thou once more
  In death deliver me.

Thou liv'st and lovest without end,
  And dost perform Thy word;
My passing soul I now commend
  To Thee, my God and Lord!

HILLER.

1765.

* * * * *
  * * * *
  * * *
  * *
  *

BLESSED ARE THE DEAD WHICH
DIE IN THE LORD.

REV. XIV. 13.

for the

Burial of the Dead.

FOR

HE THAT IS

DEAD IS FREED

FROM SIN; NOW IF

WE BE DEAD WITH CHRIST,

WE BELIEVE THAT WE

SHALL ALSO LIVE

WITH HIM.

REV E.

XIV.

13.

For the Burial
of the Dead.

I.

Now hush your cries, and shed no tear,
On such death none should look with fear;
He died a faithful Christian man,
And with his death true life began.

Coffin and grave we deck with care,
His body reverently we bear,
It is not dead but rests in God,
And softly sleeps beneath the sod.

It seems as all were over now,—
The heavy limbs, the soulless brow,—
Yet through these rigid limbs once more
A nobler life, ere long, shall pour.

These dead dry bones again shall feel
New warmth and vigour through them steal :
Reknit and living they shall soar,
On high where Christ lives evermore.

This body, lying stiff and stark,
Shall rise unharm'd from out the dark,
And swiftly mount up through the skies,
Even as the spirit heavenwards flies.

The buried grain of wheat must die,
Wither'd and worthless long must lie,
Yet springs to light all sweet and fair,
And proper fruits shall richly bear :

Even so this body made of dust,
To earth we once again entrust,
And painless it shall slumber here,
Until the Last Great Day appear.

God breathed into this house of clay
The spirit that hath pass'd away,
Christ gave the true courageous mind,
The noble heart, ye no more find.

Now earth has hid it from our eyes,
Till God shall bid it wake and rise,
Who ne'er the creature will forget,
On whom His image He hath set.

Ah, would that promised Day were here,
When Christ shall once again appear ;
When He shall call, nor one be lost,
To endless life earth's buried host !

N. HERMANN. 1560.
After Prudentius.

II.

OW rests her soul in Jesu's arms,
 Her body in the grave sleeps well,
His heart her death-chill'd heart re-warms,
 And rest more deep than tongue can tell,
Her few brief hours of conflict pass'd,—
She finds with Christ, her Friend, at last ;
She bathes in tranquil seas of peace,
 God wipes away her tears, she feels
 New life that all her languor heals,
The glory of the Lamb she sees.

She hath escaped all danger now,
 Her pain and sighing all are fled ;
The crown of joy is on her brow,
 Eternal glories o'er her shed,
In golden robes, a queen, a bride,
She standeth at her Sovereign's side,
She sees His face unveil'd and bright ;
 With joy and love He greets her soul,
 She feels herself made inly whole,
A lesser light amid His light.

The child hath now its Father seen,
 And feels what kindling love may be,
And knoweth what those words may mean.
 "Himself, the Father, loveth thee."
A shoreless ocean, an abyss
Unfathom'd, fill'd with good and bliss,

Now breaks on her enraptured sight ;
  She sees God's face, she learneth there
  What this shall be, to be His heir,
Joint-heir with Christ her Lord, in light.

The body rests, its labours over,
  And sleeps till Christ shall bid it wake ;
The dust that earth and darkness cover,
  Then as a sun its tomb shall break.
Ah, with what joy it rises then
To meet the perfect soul again !
Redeem'd from death, no more to sever,
  At that great marriage feast shall they
  With all the saints their homage pay,
And worship there the Lamb for ever.

We who yet wander through the waste,
  In faith long after Thee on high ;
While here the bread of tears we taste,
  We think upon that home of joy,
Where we (who knows how soon ?) shall meet
With all the saints at Jesu's feet,
And dwell with Him for ever there.
  We shall see God ; how deep the bliss
  We know not yet that lies in this ;
Lord Jesus, come, our hearts prepare !

ALLENDORF.

1725.

III.

O how blessed, faithful souls, are ye,
Who have pass'd through death; your God ye see,
    Escaped at last
From all the sorrows that yet hold us fast!

Here as in a prison we are bound,
Care and fear, and terrors hem us round,
    And all we know
It is but toil and grief of heart below.

While that ye are resting in your home,
Safe from pain, all misery o'ercome,
    No grief or cross
Can mix with yonder joys to work you loss.

Christ doth wipe away your every tear,
Ye possess what we but long for here,
    To you is sung
The song that ne'er through mortal ears hath rung.

Who is there that would not gladly die,
Changing earth for such a home on high,
    Or who would stay
To toil amid these sorrows night and day?

Come, O Christ, release us from our post,
Lead us quickly hence to yonder host,
    Whose battle won,
Now drink in joy and bliss from Thee our Sun.

SIMON DACH. 1650.

INDEX.

The numbers on the left hand are the numbers of the original Hymns in the "Versuch eines allgemeinen Gesang und Gebet Buchs," from which these Hymns are translated.

INDEX.

INDEX.

* No. 73 in the smaller collection.

TABLE OF GERMAN HYMNS.

TABLE OF GERMAN HYMNS.

TABLE OF GERMAN HYMNS.

TABLE OF GERMAN HYMNS.

TO

THE END

THAT MY GLORY MAY
SING PRAISE TO
THEE & NOT
BE SILENT.
PS. XXX, 12.

www.ingramcontent.com/pod-product-compliance
Lightning Source LLC
Chambersburg PA
CBHW020854020726
47497CB00005B/1398